THE CURE

A VICTORIA ASHER NOVEL

ANNALISA GRANT

For Claire.

You are braver than you know.

"She believed she could,
so she did."

THE CURE

Prologue

I should have been more alarmed by the amount of bio hazardous waste I was elbow deep in, but years of emptying trash into the bins behind The Clock Diner prepared me for the weird and grossly disturbing. What a fine initiation into my life as a Rogue agent.

Steps echoed in the hall. Initially, I assumed it was Ian and Carter returning from the ass kicking they had been giving, but the sound was off. They both wore military type boots. The shoes moving toward me were some kind of sneaker, and the wearer shuffled one foot as he walked. More importantly, there was only one person headed my way.

I gave the container one last look and made sure my gun was ready. "Nothing here," I said as I stood. I whipped my gun up swiftly and pointed it at the man standing before me in a lab coat. "Freeze," I instructed. It wasn't as commanding as I had practiced in the mirror, but at least Carter wasn't there to point out how weak I sounded.

Stunned, the man turned on his heels and sped down the hall. I fired once, and splinters exploded from the doorframe. I followed him out into the hall in time to see him enter the stairwell. By the time I reached the stairs, he was already a flight ahead. I fired at him again, and this time the bullet dinged off the metal railing. "Dammit!"

I took the stairs two at a time and followed him up and outside, then down a street to the left of the building. He was fast. The distance between us grew. I increased my pace, and my lungs began to burn. I pumped my arms, the weight of my gun giving me an extra workout. He looked back a few times with a sinister smile spread across his face.

"Victoria," Ian's voice said sternly through my earpiece. "Where are you?"

Crap.

It wasn't until then that I thought to press the button on my earpiece.

"Um…." I stuttered as I ran.

"Are you panting?" he asked.

I took four seconds to contemplate what I was going to say. Ian was sure to be furious that I took off without a single word, especially after he ordered me to stay put.

What the hell. He's already pissed!

"I've got one! He bolted out the west side door," I said breathlessly. "Take the first street to the left."

"Bloody hell, Victoria!"

Yep. He's pissed.

"Stay put! We're coming." Ian declared.

I couldn't stay put. Someone with answers we desperately needed was getting away, and I couldn't let that happen.

The man disappeared down an alley. I ran faster, afraid he would enter one of the buildings and then I'd never find him. I rounded the corner and was immediately clotheslined across the chest. My bones rattled as I landed hard on my back. When my hand slammed to the ground, my gun flew from my grip and rocketed under a parked car. In a flash he was over me, grabbing and lifting me by my jacket. As I struggled to gain my footing, he released one hand long enough to backhand me across the face. I tasted blood. That's when I jabbed my knee into his crotch. He released me and doubled over, so I kneed him in the face, too.

I dove to the ground and went for my gun. My arm stretched as far as it could under the car, and I willed my fingers to be a quarter-inch longer. I almost had it when two fists grasped my ankles and dragged me across the pavement. I flipped over, pressed my feet into his chest, and shoved as hard as I could. He was strong and heavy, laying his weight against me, but I managed to push hard enough to make him stumble back. I didn't have time to go for my gun again, so I jumped to my feet and tried to recall every hand-to-hand combat technique Ian and Adam taught me, as well as a few from my trusty YouTube videos.

First, I knuckled him in the throat. He choked and coughed right before he rammed into me like linebacker, crashing us into a car. When he came at me again, I slid to the side and used his own force to smash his head into the car window. Thinking I bought enough time, I went for my gun again. Mistake. He grabbed me from behind, his arm across my chest. I lifted my knees to my chest and shoved off of the car door. He stumbled back and fell to the ground, allowing me to roll backward and out of his grasp. Before he could stand, I jabbed my foot into his nose. When he reached for his face, I gave him one more jolt to the crotch for good measure. Blood poured from his nose as he writhed in pain on the asphalt.

I dropped next to the car, slid a leg under the body where my gun was hiding, and kicked it closer. Gun in hand, I stood over my assailant with the barrel pointed at him. I was about to question him when Ian's voice barked in my ear.

"Victoria! Where are you?" His anger hadn't dissipated.

I pressed my earpiece. "I'm in an alley about sixty yards off the first street I followed him down. On the right," I told him. With my gun still pointed at my opponent, I waited for my tongue lashing from Ian. My heart raced with excitement. I couldn't wait for Ian to see how I had handled myself.

"You'll regret this," the man said, rasping in an English accent, as he rose to his knees and then to his feet.

"The only thing I regret is how difficult I've made it for you to speak. You have a lot of questions to answer," I told him. "Now put your hands behind your head." I finally had a chance to examine my attacker. To describe him as taller than me was unnecessary, as everyone but small children are taller than me. He had typical features, nothing that set him apart from any average-looking guy. But with his hands behind his head, his arms were now exposed. He had a single tattoo on the inside of his forearm. It was exactly like the one I had seen earlier. The shading and design were so realistic that it appeared to almost jump off of his skin.

"Vic!" Carter's voice echoed off the buildings towering around us.

"It's too late," my opponent muttered. "It's too late for all of us. The clock is ticking."

My brows knit together. "What did you say?"

The words had barely left my lips when I was grabbed from behind. My assailant pulled my elbows together behind my back and snatched my gun from me. My head turned enough to see that it was another man, wearing scrubs just like the man lying on the ground in front of me.

I felt something sharp against my neck. Ian yelling was the last thing I heard.

Chapter 1

Blades of grass tickled between my toes as I laid my head in Ian's lap and stared up at the Eiffel Tower. We'd picnicked in this place every day since we arrived in Paris seven days before. Our time in Spain had been tiring with all the climbing up and down that was required if you wanted to be anywhere near the water. So when Ian told me the last stop on our sabbatical tour was France, I made him promise it would be exciting but restful. After all, I would be headed into full-fledged Rogue training when we got back to London.

"Do we really have to leave tomorrow?" I asked in a relaxed haze.

"I'm afraid so." Ian brushed away the hair that had blown into my face. "Aren't you looking forward to getting settled into your new flat?"

I chuckled. "You mean the flat that you *stole* for me?"

"I didn't steal it!" he protested with a smirk. "I merely suggested that the Frys would be happier if they retired to West Malling sooner rather than later."

"And then you gave them the £25,000 they still had left to save before they could move."

"Anything to keep you close." Ian smiled and kissed my forehead.

Close was an understatement. The Frys' flat was one floor below Ian's in a building just three blocks from INTERPOL's Marsham Street office in London. While the UK headquarters were in Manchester, the powers that be decided an office in London would be smart after a rise in acts of terrorism in the city.

I sat up and let out a heavy sigh.

"Are you all right?" Ian asked.

I nodded. "I'm scared out of my mind, but I'm all right."

Ian took my hand in his, brushing his thumb across my knuckles. "You're going to be brilliant. I believe in you."

"Thank you." I took a deep breath and shook my head. "Okay. We've been here for hours, and I am now officially hungry ... again." I slid my shoes back on before I stood and dusted off the seat of my pants.

"So demanding!" Ian laughed as he stood.

"I am not demanding!" I objected. "I require only two things: feed me and tell me I'm pretty."

"That I can do, Miss Asher." Ian wrapped his arms around my waist and pulled me to him. He pressed his mouth to mine and possessed me in one smooth move. Our lips moved together with care and precision as I ran my fingers through Ian's blonde hair and cupped the back of his neck. His hands found their way to my backside twice before jerking back to my waist. When I had been sufficiently kissed, Ian pulled away and took my face in his hands. "How did I ever exist without you?"

I smiled softly. "You got along just fine without me."

"My life was mediocre at best," he said. "Victoria ... there's something I've wanted to talk with you about. Well, really, something I've wanted to say."

"Let's walk. I'm starved!" I picked up the paper bag left from our lunch hours earlier and walked quickly to a trash bin on the path at the perimeter of the grass. I tossed it in and turned to wait for Ian. I plastered a huge smile on my face. "Where to, boss?"

"So I'm *boss* now?" He raised an eyebrow at me suspiciously.

I shrugged and began to stroll. "Just thought I'd see how it sounded since that'll be who you are to me in a few days."

Ian threaded his fingers through mine. We were silent for a while, both of us seemingly unsure what to say next. I was excited about being a Rogue agent. But there was so much to be nervous about. I had been brought on because of my ability to notice things others didn't. I fared well during Adam's fast-track training outside Bologna, but the expectations for my performance were low to nonexistent then. How would I handle the complete Rogue training? Moreover, how would Ian and I handle it together? It was one thing when I was an obstinate sister refusing to leave the country without my brother. It was sure to be another thing to ask Ian and the rest of the team to trust their lives to my instincts as an actual member of the team.

If I were honest though, the thing that worried me the most was my relationship with Ian. I wasn't concerned that we wouldn't make it through training. He was going to be relentless, but I felt certain we could survive his cracking the whip. I was concerned about what would happen once we got into the field. Would I be able to let him do his job knowing he might not come back? Could he do the same for me? I didn't want to give Director Thatcher any reason to separate us, but if the logistics of being in a relationship with my superior was on my radar, it was surely on hers.

"It doesn't change anything, Victoria," Ian finally said.

"I know you believe that," I replied.

Ian stopped us in front of a small market. "I have confidence in you, and you have confidence in me. We trust each other. Don't we?"

"It's not about trust, Ian. It's about…"

"It's about what?"

"It's about when we're not together in the safety of the training center or even at a safe house. Am I going to be able to do my job knowing that you're out there somewhere having God only knows what happen to you? I'll never get the image of you hanging from that rafter out of my head. And are you going to be able to send me out to do my job? As I recall, you weren't thrilled about my little mission with Carter that night in Padova."

Ian drew in a cleansing breath and put his hands on his hips. "It sounds like you've been thinking this through."

"It's not thinking, Ian. It's worrying," I said softly. "I've lost everyone I love. I don't know what I'd do if I lost you, too. And I'm scared because I don't know that I'm ever going to be a strong enough agent to say goodbye to you."

"You're not going to have to say goodbye to me." Ian's face was pained.

"Do you know that for certain?" I challenged. His eyes dropped.

"Here's what I do know," he began. "I know that training is going to be difficult. I know that you're going to be a spectacular agent. I know that, because of you, my life will never be the same." Ian took my chin in his hand. "I also know that how I feel about you makes me even more determined to come back from every mission in one piece because I *never* want you to feel that kind of loss again."

I felt the same way, and it made me just as determined to be the best agent I could be. I was resolute in my decision to train as hard, if not harder, than any agent out there. I would be such a strong agent that Ian would never fear for my survival, and Director Thatcher would never second guess agreeing to bring me on and place me on Ian's team.

"Thank you." I pushed up on my toes and kissed Ian softly on the lips.

"Why do I feel like your mind isn't completely at ease?" he asked with a raised eyebrow.

"Because you're good at your job." I gave him a thin smile. "Listen, it's going to take time, and I have to be okay with that. Two months ago, I was waiting tables in Miami. Today I'm standing in the shadow of the Eiffel Tower with you. I'm going to work hard, Ian, but you have to cut me some slack on the adjustment period. Okay?"

Ian smiled. "Okay."

"Great!" I flipped my demeanor and my hair around and grabbed Ian's hand. We continued walking past the little market and came upon a specialty grocer. The window had an entire display of American food. "OH. MY. GOD. Is that Lucky Charms? We have to go in!" I dragged Ian into the little shop and found the aisle that contained some of the foods I hadn't realized I missed. One by one, I picked up items and shoved them into Ian's arms. "Oreos! Cinnamon Toast Crunch! And the Holy Grail of food groups: peanut butter! Seriously? What is it with Europeans and peanut butter? You'll eat that black tar, Marmite, but not delicious peanut butter?"

Ian laughed. "Hey! I like peanut butter ... sort of."

"Sort of? Okay, your moderate appreciation for peanut butter is a deep dark secret you've been keeping from me. Which makes me wonder what else I don't know about you." Actually, there was a lot I didn't know about Ian. We had only known each other for a couple of months, and for the first month we were in almost constant peril. "I have an idea."

I snatched a few more necessities off the shelf, Ian paid, and we went back to the flat Ian rented for us just a few blocks away. While we ate peanut butter toast and sugary cereal, I introduced Ian to a game Tiffany and I used to play.

"Please tell me your people have heard of Thumb War," I declared.

"Ha! Yes, I've heard of that," he said with a laugh.

"Good! Here's how it works: we play Thumb War. Whoever loses has to tell the winner a secret."

"Sounds easy enough. And, comparing the sizes of our hands, I'm feeling pretty confident." Ian cocked his head and gave me the side eye.

"We'll just see about that!" I took a bite of peanut butter toast and extended my hand. Within three seconds Ian had won the first round. He laughed with joy at his victory. "All right, all right. Tiffany always won the first rounds, too, but I'm the comeback kid, so watch out."

"Do I get to decide what I want to know?" Ian rubbed his hands together in anticipation.

"Nope! They're secrets, so each person gets to decide what they want to tell. I'm going to start this out on a super sexy note." I winked. "I wet the bed until I was four."

"I don't know what they taught you in America, but that is *not* sexy."

Round after round, Ian won. And round after round I told Ian some of my funniest and most embarrassing secrets.

"My first kiss was awful. He rolled his tongue around in my mouth like was hunting for something. So gross."

"When I was 15, I split my pants at my first job interview."

"When I'm lost, I become enraged. Completely unhinged! Actually, this might be the most important thing you learn about me."

After an hour of painful loss, I finally won.

"You gave me that win, but I don't even care." I lifted my arms in triumph. "Soooooo?"

Ian pushed the plates and bowls from the end of the table where we sat. Then he took my hands, directing me to stand with him. "My secret is that I want nothing more than to kiss you right now." Without missing a beat, Ian leaned in and began kissing my neck.

"Um," I squeaked out. "That's not a secret. I'm fully aware that you want to kiss me all the time. You suck at this game."

"Shhh."

Ian lifted me up and sat me on the end of the table. He pulled at the bottom of my shirt and ran his hands against the smooth skin of my back. Electricity surged through me. I wrapped my legs around him and pulled him closer to me. I couldn't get enough of him. His mouth covered mine and we devoured each other like our lives depended on it. Ian drew me even closer and pulled me from the table, carrying me toward the bedroom. Once at the door, he stopped and lowered me to the floor. He took my face in his hands and kissed me hard, even biting my lip at one point.

Then he pulled away.

Breathless, we stood there, locked on each other, my heart galloping inside my chest.

And, just as he had every night since our sabbatical had begun, Ian whispered, "Goodnight, Victoria."

And, just as I had responded each time, I sighed, "Goodnight, Ian."

I took a deep breath and kissed him one last time before I closed the bedroom door.

Lying in bed, I considered the days to come. We would leave Paris the next day and go home to London. *Home*. It was strange to think of London as my home. We had only spent a week there securing a place for me to live before Ian whisked me away. *Ian*. I smiled. It wasn't about London or Spain or even Paris. It was about Ian. Home was wherever he was. In a matter of days, I'd begin my official training as a Rogue agent, and no matter what I had to do, I would do my best to always make it *home*.

Chapter 2

Sweat rolled from my forehead into my eye. Rapid blinking did nothing to relieve the stinging, so I lowered my body and rubbed the discomfort away.

"If you drop again, I'm adding another 30 seconds," Ian said firmly. I had been propped up on my forearms and toes for what seemed like eternity. In reality, it had been less than a minute. That planking business was no joke.

"It's the first day, Ian. You can't cut me a little slack?" I argued.

"No," he said sternly. "You wanted to be treated like every other agent, so that's what I'm doing."

I propped myself back up. "Adam never made me do anything like this," I grunted.

"Adam gave you just enough training to defend yourself. My job is to make sure you stay alive *and* take down your assailant," Ian insisted. "In order to do that, your core must be strong."

I grunted again and pushed through, counting to myself in sets of ten.

One, two, three, four five, six, seven, eight, nine, ten.
Two, two, three, four five, six, seven, eight, nine, ten.
Three, two, three, four five, six, seven, eight, nine, ten.

We held that plank for three of the longest minutes of my life.

"Now, on your back. Sit-ups. One minute. As many as you can."

"Wait. What?" I collapsed on the ground and rolled onto my back, grateful to leave a position Satan himself must have created.

"As many as you can," he reiterated. "As long as it's at least 38."

"That is oddly specific."

"We use a scoring system as a guideline for physical fitness. You get zero or negative points for anything less than thirty-eight sit-ups in one minute," he explained.

"I hate you."

******

"What's this?" I asked. We had driven out of the city to a field similar to the one Adam had hunted me down in. There were two rows of three posts, each with a red flag atop it, and the rows were at a fair distance from the other.

"300 meter dash," Ian answered.

"How fast?" In the weeks I had been training, I'd learned that each task had a score attached to it. Planks, burpees, and squats: they all seemed to have a requirement that only served to prove my ineptness in physical fitness. I was getting stronger everyday, increasing my score in small increments, but running was another story. I couldn't get my heart and lungs on board with cardiovascular exercise. I used to tell my best friend Tiffany that if she ever saw me running, she should run too, because it meant that someone was probably chasing me. Now that I was a Rogue agent, my desire to not get shot and die was surely what would keep me going.

I ran with Ian every morning before going in for training. I tried to keep up with him, but his pace was ridiculous. He had to force himself to slow down so he didn't leave me in his dust. My initiation run was five miles and took me almost two hours. Ian wasn't even the slightest bit out of breath, while I was sweating like a horse and begging for sweet death to take me.

"51.1 seconds."

"Well, shit."

"Running will be one of your most important skills." Ian said that to me at least every other morning. "Whether you're running to something or away from it, your pace will determine your fate."

"Right. So no pressure." I put my hands on my hips and took a cleansing breath as I sized up my new nemesis.

We walked to the first post, and Ian pointed across the field. "To that post and back is 300 meters. Get to the other side, grab the flag, and return."

"In no more than 51.1 seconds. That's cool. I've got this." I smirked.

Ian brought his wrist up and nodded, pinching the sides of his watch. I took off running, pumping my arms hard, as if that was going to give me lightening fast feet. Reaching the other side, I snatched the flag from the top and boomeranged myself around the post and back toward my starting line. I practically tackled Ian upon my arrival.

Bent over with my hands on my knees, I gasped for air. "So?"

"55.2," Ian said soberly.

I breathed in through my nose and out through my mouth, calming my heart rate. Then I walked to the next post and looked at Ian. "Again."

"Victoria, you can catch your breath," Ian admonished. "You don't have to jump right in. It's okay."

"It's not okay. You think Damon and his goons are going to give me a minute to catch my breath?"

Ian looked at me sternly. "Victoria…"

"Don't *Victoria* me, Ian. One day we'll find Damon, and I'm *going* to take him down. If that's the driving force behind me pushing myself to be stronger and faster … then just let me have this. At least for now. Okay?"

Ian made a thin line of his lips. "All right then. Again."

******

Scant plumes of smoke rose from my gun as I fired another magazine at the target. This was the one area of my training that I felt confident in. Adam had been an amazing teacher, but it had been a while since I'd held a gun, so I beat Ian by an hour to the range in the training facility to get in some practice.

When Ian walked in, he raised an eyebrow at me.

"I'm not cheating. I'm just getting some extra practice in," I said preemptively.

"I'm happy to see you here already. And I expect you to be getting extra practice in for *all* of your training," he smiled.

"Of course! I'm *totally* going to go for an extra run later." I hit the button to retrieve my target. When it arrived along the track system at my station, I received a disapproving look from Ian.

"I appreciate your skill in hitting the target with a fair level of accuracy, but we make it a policy to not *aim* for the head of our subjects," he said. "And the fact that you have a picture of Damon's face attached to the target…"

"Don't, Ian."

"I was going to say that, well, I suppose everyone needs a little motivation."

******

"C'mon, slowpoke!" I called to Ian. I rounded the corner and stopped in front of our building. When he finally appeared, I threw my hands in the air Rocky style and jogged around in victory. It had taken three months, but I beat him.

"Well done," Ian said through heavy breaths.

"I know you let me win," I said. "It's not like three miles in 33 minutes is an Olympic pace."

"It's not a competition, Victoria."

"Like hell it's not! You've been pushing me for months to do better, be better. You're the only benchmark I have, Ian. My goal is always to do as well as or better than you."

"You've trained hard, and your victory today is well deserved." Ian kissed me chastely on the mouth and then jogged up the steps to the entrance of our building. I watched as he opened the door for me. "Are you coming?"

"Yeah, no. My legs are Jell-O. You're going to have to carry me."

Ian gave a hearty laugh and came down the steps to get me. He flung me over his shoulder like a sack of potatoes. I let out an excited squeal, but the crying aches of my body wouldn't be silent either, and a groan escaped my lips as well. Ian gently lowered me onto my couch in the new place I called home. It was small, as most flats in London are. The kitchen was large enough for only a table for two. I had a small sofa and a single wingback chair in the living room where Ian had mounted a TV on the wall above the fireplace. The guest bedroom was sparsely furnished with just a single bed. But my bedroom was like a sanctuary. Plush bedding on the most comfortable mattress ever and battleship gray paint on the walls.

Ian stood above me and smiled sweetly as he shook his head. "You're something, you know that?"

"Are my thighs supposed to burn like this?"

Ian laughed. "You're the one who decided to sprint the last half mile!" He leaned down and kissed the top of my head before moving into the kitchen. Glasses clanking and the sound of water being poured echoed into the living room. Ian returned and handed me a glass of cool water. I gulped it down like my life depended on it.

"Oh, thank you!" I sighed.

"I'm going to go shower and get ready," Ian said. "Be ready in an hour?"

"I don't think I'm going to be able to move for an hour." I winced as I attempted to shift my seat. "Do we really have to go out tonight?"

"You're adorable." Ian snickered. "And yes, we do. You've accomplished so much in your training, and you deserve a celebratory dinner."

"Can't we celebrate here … where I don't have to move and you can wait on me hand and foot?" I spread a cheesy grin across my face.

Ian sat down next to me and took my hand in his.

"We'll be back in the field soon, and I'd like to have as much normal time together as we can," he said softly.

"Sounds like *you've* been thinking things through," I said. He nodded and I sighed. "Are you regretting asking me to stay?"

"No," he said quickly. "I'm realizing that that you were right: I may have to say goodbye to you one day. That's the nature of this job. And we can be determined to come back from every mission in one piece, but I can't promise that either of us will. But what's killing me is the thought that my death will just be another person on your list. Another person who left you behind."

"Here's what *I* know," I began. "I know that training has been more challenging than I ever imagined. I know that you're an incredible trainer and a spectacular agent. And I know that, because of *you*, my life will never be the same. I can sit here and dwell on the pain and loss that I've endured, shake my fist at the sky, and ask God why. Or I can accept the fact that everything, even the shitty stuff, happens for a reason. I don't want to lose you, ever, not to anything. But don't ever think that you'd be just another name on a list. You will never be *just* an anything to me, Ian Hale."

Ian took my face in his hand and ran his thumb across my cheek. "I had planned on doing this tonight at dinner, but seeing as it appears we're in for the night..." he began. "I have something I need to say. It's been begging to be let loose for weeks now, but it can't wait any longer."

Ian took in a deep breath and I seemed to lose all of mine. I knew what he was about to say. I was excited and scared at once. I both wanted him to say the words and needed him to keep it locked up just a bit longer. I was fully aware of my feelings for Ian but unsure I could utter the actual words. Being a Rogue agent seemed much less scary.

I couldn't cut him off. Not again. So, I smiled and then bit my lip in anticipation.

"Victoria ... I love you."

Chapter 3

My chest burned from the cold air I inhaled while I ran at what felt like an inhuman pace. She was behind me, gaining fast. I ditched her once before, but she found me again. I had no choice but to turn the tables on her. *She* had to become the target, and I *had* to get a hit. I tried not to look back, but I had a bad habit of making that mistake. She looked right at me, aimed her gun, and shot. I turned down another hall in the nick of time. I cut the corner too short and slammed my shoulder into the wall. My arm throbbed from the jolt.

I needed to get far enough ahead to get into position where I could ambush her. It felt like an impossible task in the winding maze of hallways of the abandoned office building, but adrenaline and the burning desire to beat her ass to the ground turned my feet into rockets. I found a fire exit and took the stairs two at a time, racing harder and faster than I ever had before. I watched the floor numbers increase with every level I conquered.

Thirteen.

Fourteen.

Fifteen.

Sixteen.

The door below me slammed open, the bang echoing like church bells. I looked down and saw her charging the stairs. Her dark hair whipped around like a shampoo commercial, making me despise her even more for chasing me and looking good while doing it. She was better and faster than I could ever be. After three months of training with Ian, though, I was ready for this. I pushed harder than I had before, but the pace at which she took the stairs made me question my fate.

I gained more ground when I made it to the roof before she hit the fifteenth floor. The stairwell had been dimly lit, and the sun scorched my corneas as soon I crossed the threshold into the light. It took me seconds longer than I could afford to adjust. I managed to make it behind one of the two huge structures that housed the air conditioning units for the building. I had just positioned myself on the concrete pad that surrounded the structure when the heavy, metal door closed with a crash behind me. I had less than a minute before my opponent would appear. No more than sixty seconds before I found out if this would be the end for me.

The door opened slowly with a grinding whine. With my back to the wall, I peeked around the corner and saw her gun make an appearance through the door first. I checked my gun again to make sure it was fully loaded and ready. It was ready, but was I?

"Victoria." Her singsong voice calling my name made me cringe. I hated when people used my full name. Except Ian. I loved the way my name sounded coming from his lips. "Come out, come out, wherever you are."

I closed my eyes and listened to her footsteps. It was hard to hear at first because my heart was beating so loudly. The adrenaline coursing through my body made blood rush through my ears like a train.

I had to focus on the skill set that made Ian and Director Thatcher want to keep me on a Rogue team: I was incredibly observant. I may not have been at my physical peak, but I had better eyes, ears, and intuition than the average person. I took a deep breath and listened again.

Her feet crunched the gravel rooftop. The sound echoed off the second structure, cluing me into the direction she had chosen to take. *My right. She's coming around from my right.* I rolled gently to my left and stood, readying my weapon. I turned the corner and walked softly on the outer edges of my feet as I watched her disappear to the place I had just been hiding. Staying on the concrete path, I raised my weapon and followed her with trepidation.

"Drop your weapon," I commanded.

She turned around slowly with her hands in surrender and looked at me sympathetically. "Oh, Vic. I'm sorry, but you didn't win this time."

"What are you talking about? I have you, Claudia," I said confidently.

"Do you?" a voice rang from behind me. "Drop *your* weapon."

I turned around. "What the hell, Ian?" I lowered my arms in defeat and clenched my teeth in anger. I had come so far in this training exercise, farther than I ever had before, only to have Ian set me up for failure?

"You can never assume your target is alone. Just because you don't see a second or third assailant doesn't mean they aren't there," he explained.

This was the tenth mock encounter I had done since I started with Rogue. In between my physical training every day, I was put in a scenario every week where I had to capture my opponent. Claudia had just returned from a short assignment in Washington and volunteered for the training. "It'll be so fun!" she said.

Yeah. Fun.

"You sent me in alone. How was I to know you'd be here? There has never been a second subject! You ambushed me, Ian." I stormed to the stairwell and flew down each step much faster than I had climbed them.

"You can't be mad at him, Vic," Claudia said as she caught up with me. Ian kept his distance. "There's never going to be an ideal scenario. It's not like you can turn to the other guy and say 'Oh, you're not supposed to be here. I'm only prepared to seize *one* subject. Thanks!'"

"If I had known there was a chance of there being someone else up there, I would have changed my tactic, Claudia." I picked up my pace and strode down to the tunnel that connected the training building to INTERPOL's main office. Three miles separated the training building and main office, so INTERPOL took over an old tube line and stocked both sides with golf carts. Three miles doesn't sound like much, but when you're in a taxi in the heart of London, it can take a while.

I zoomed down the line, fuming. I had spent countless hours over the last three months working my ass off to feel even the slightest bit worthy of Director Thatcher's confidence in me. Every target I hit, every scenario I dissected, every clue I uncovered … somehow it all seemed like it was for nothing.

I knew Ian was going to continue to push me as hard as he had during my initial training, but I couldn't help but think that today's ambush had more to do with the fact that I hadn't said those three magical words back to him.

I charged into the small firing range in the basement of the building like a woman on a mission. I preferred this range to the massive one in the training facility. I scanned my card that logged all the comings and goings of everyone and waited for the door to unlock. The ammo guy,

Thomas, knew what I wanted and had it ready for me as soon as he buzzed me in. I unloaded the blanks that my gun held for training, and replaced the magazine with the real thing.

Taking my favorite spot at the last booth in the row next to the wall, I took several deep breaths while I waited for the target to travel to the end of my lane. I fired off the first round slowly as I always did. The first one always got me. After that I blew through two magazines quickly, hitting the chest of my target every time. I had gotten so much better than that first night at the old factory outside Bologna. That first night ... I'd been so sore. And exhilarated.

I was about to buzz the intercom to ask Thomas for more ammo when Ian entered the range.

"Nice to see you haven't put *my* picture on the head," he said. He was wearing his signature black pants and white dress shirt with the top two buttons undone. His sleeves were still rolled up from when he ambushed me on the roof. I hated that I still found him irresistibly attractive when I was angry with him.

"I tried, but they wouldn't let me," I snarled before I finished unloading my gun into the chest of my target. I was so furious at Ian I didn't know how to form the words to yell at him.

"You did well today, Victoria," he said calmly. He leaned against the wall behind me and crossed one ankle over the other. He was always so smooth.

"Did I? Because it looked like you were setting me up to fail." I released the magazine and did the requisite check to make sure the chamber of my gun was empty before I all but slammed it down on the counter in front of me.

"I did *not* set you up to fail. Not telling you I would be there was a part of your training. We have focused on single-assailant training for months; it was time to step up your game," he explained. "We'll do some training exercises with multiple assailants and consider adding that component again to your next training exercise."

"We'll *consider* adding it? Why? Because I failed so miserably today?"

"You know I don't think that. What is this really about?" Ian reached his hand out and brushed down the side of my arm.

I gritted my teeth, hesitant to tell him what I really thought was going on. Several heated breaths later I spat it out.

"It felt like retaliation."

"Retaliation for what?" His furrowed brow told me I had stumped him.

I swallowed hard. "For not … for not saying *it* back to you yet."

Ian shook his head. "You think I formatted the exercise to get back at you?"

"I don't know what to think." I stepped out of the booth and leaned against the wall. The pained expression on Ian's face, and the tone that matched, made me realize how silly my assumption was.

"I told you I loved you six days and"—he looked at his watch—"17 hours ago. Does it sting that you haven't returned the sentiment? Yes. Do I *want* to hear you say the words? More than I could express. But I'm not going to push you, Victoria. And I'm not going to retaliate. I'd like to think you know me better than that." He shoved his hands in his pockets. The pain on his face turned to disappointment.

"I'm sorry," I said sheepishly. "I feel really dumb for even thinking that you would do that." I stepped closer to Ian.

"You should." His voice almost barked with agitation. "I would never bring our personal life into the agency like that."

"I know, and I'm sorry." I ran my fingers from the top of my head down through my hair in frustration. "I failed, and I didn't like that. You know how important it is to me that I succeed in my training like everyone else. I'm never going to be prepared to take Damon down if I don't," I continued.

"We've talked about this. That shouldn't be your focus, Victoria," Ian said in the same stern voice he used every time my passion for going after Damon came up.

"Don't you care that this is important to me?"

He pushed off the wall and stepped closer to me. "I care about everything concerning you, but my job is to prepare you to be a skilled agent, not a woman out for vengeance."

"I can do this, Ian," I told him.

"I know you can," he said softly.

"Do you?"

"Yes, but…" Ian let out a strong rush of air. "I see the same fire in your eyes that was in Gil's when I met him, and I have to say it's a little alarming. He was set on avenging Maria's murder, and look where that got him. Now, you know I can appreciate the burning desire to right wrongs, but you're here to do more than take down the man responsible for your brother's death. If you truly want to be as successful as everyone else, then your focus has to be on being the best agent you can be for this division.

"Being ready for the field means more than being a great shot, or in your case, incredibly observant. It means going out there and focusing on your assignment, no matter what it is. If you're focused on finding Damon, you'll never be concentrated on the task before you, and that puts you and everyone on your team at risk." Slightly defeated, I lowered my head, but Ian took my chin between his fingers and lifted it. "And I *need* you to make it out alive. Every time."

"I can do this, Ian," I reiterated. "I just want to prove to you that I'm ready."

"I'd be more concerned about proving yourself to me." Director Thatcher's words echoed through the shooting range, rattling us both. She took five determined steps toward us. Ian dropped his hand from my chin and we both took a step back. He straightened his posture and put his game face on. Considering Thatcher held both our careers in her hands, the next words out of her mouth could have been for my immediate dismissal. Our relationship was no secret, but we had been very careful not to put it on display. She didn't fire me, but what she did say took me a little by surprise.

"I need you both to come with me. You've got your first assignment, Miss Asher."

Chapter 4

It was a long, anxiety-filled walk to Director Thatcher's office. I was so sure she was changing her mind about me staying, every stilettoed step she took rattled me. She may have been beautiful, but tough as nails didn't even begin to describe her.

One night over a bottle of wine Ian, gave me the skinny on Penny Thatcher. Like him, she had been a Green Beret. She saw her fair share of combat and became a Rogue agent after her husband was killed in action. She worked her way up with INTERPOL and had been Director of the Rogue Division for five years.

I hadn't spent very much time with Thatcher since I came to INTERPOL. Certainly not enough to ascertain by her words or tone if Ian and I were in for a tongue lashing before being given our assignment. She was an extremely guarded and by the book person. Exactly the type one would expect to run a secret agent organization.

"Would you like some tea?" Thatcher asked politely as we all sat, she behind her beautifully ornate desk, Ian and I in the wingback chairs that faced her.

"No, thank you," I replied.

"Why don't we just get to the task at hand? You said there was an assignment." Ian leaned back in his chair and crossed his ankle over his knee. He had the uncanny ability to flip a switch between the soft and kind Ian that was my boyfriend, and the rough and tough Agent Ian Hale.

Thatcher rested her forearms on her desk with a file folder between them, her green eyes narrowing as if she were contemplating which to address first: the assignment or the display of Ian's and my relationship she had just witnessed. Finally, she turned her computer monitor to face us. On the screen was the still shot of a paused video. The picture was blurred, making it hard to clearly identify anything in the frame.

"This came to me in an email last night," she finally said as she clicked her mouse.

The video began in some kind of hospital or lab. There was a stainless steel table and a back counter with vials and tubes and everything I hated about high school chemistry. But the guy who came into the frame was more Walter White than my nerdy chemistry teacher, Mr. Miles. The man's head was shaved and he had a brown and graying goatee. And the tattoos on his arms almost made you miss the fact that he was wearing a lab coat with the sleeves rolled up.

"Penny ... I don't know where to start, so I'll just cut to the chase. I need your help. You and Geoffrey were always like family to me and, frankly, I didn't know where else to turn. The people I'm working for, this ... *lab* is not at all what I once believed it was. There's too much to go into now. All I can say is that it's gone terribly wrong.

"I've destroyed all of my research so no one can recreate the mistake I made. Once they find out what I've done, they will no doubt go after Wren to use as incentive. Please. I need you to get to her. She'll lead you to what they're looking for. She'll lead you to the antidote. There isn't much time. They're likely going to kill me. They'll certainly do it when they can't find Wren to use against me."

He finally took a breath and let it out quickly, pausing to give respect to the gravity of the situation. Fear fought for a place in his eyes, but he pushed it back like the badass his physical appearance suggested.

"Geoffrey was like a brother to me, and I have been deeply touched by our lasting friendship even after his death. I understand I am asking much of you. Please, Penny ... I need you to protect her. She's all I've got. She's all I've ever had. When this is all over, please remind her of just how much I loved her."

Thatcher clicked her mouse and turned the screen around before she looked at us again. I swallowed hard, waiting for her to speak.

"That is Jeremy Strasser," she began. "He was a medical researcher with the United States Army and is a specialist and an expert in infectious disease. My husband Geoffrey was a doctor in the British Army. They worked together on several joint projects while Jeremy was stationed in Belgium. Over the years they became great friends. He is one of the few people I've remained friends with since Geoffrey died, and I would do anything for him."

"With all due respect, I'm not interested in another babysitting assignment," Ian told her in no uncertain terms.

With a deadpan look on her face she replied, "With all due respect to you, Mr. Hale, I don't care."

"If I can ask," I began. "Who's Wren?" It took a moment for Thatcher to look at me. She and Ian were having some kind of mental showdown that she had to tear herself from.

"Wren is Jeremy's daughter. She's an art student at Oxford," Thatcher answered. Ian stayed conspicuously silent.

"So what did Strasser create, and why does there need to be an antidote?" I asked.

"That's an excellent question, and the first one I plan on asking Jeremy as soon as I see him," Thatcher answered. "But considering his expertise, I imagine it's quite dangerous." She turned her attention back to Ian and opened her mouth to speak.

Ian bolted up from his seat before she could utter a sound. "All right then. We'll go to Oxford and bring her back. Are we done?"

I breathed four times before Thatcher spoke. "Miss Asher, would give Mr. Hale and me a moment?"

My heart quickened. Why was Ian being such a jerk? Maybe he felt he had more leeway with her, but as the newest Rogue agent, I couldn't fathom taking that tone with her.

"Of course," I said. "I'll just wait outside." I stood up on rickety legs and walked to the door. I passed the threshold and into Thatcher's waiting area, waiting for the door to click behind me before I allowed myself to breathe. Millie, Thatcher's assistant, sat at her desk staring at me with narrowed eyes. Her crush on Ian was common knowledge, as was her hatred of me. I gave her a pleasant smile and sat on the couch outside Thatcher's door.

Millie's phone buzzed and she promptly answered it. "Director Thatcher's office. She's in a meeting right now. She just returned that file to me a bit ago. Yes, I'd be happy to, sir." Millie hung up the phone and swiveled her chair to the side, picked up a file from her desk, and exited to the hallway without a second glance my way.

When I was sure she was long gone, I darted up and got as close to Thatcher's door as possible. It was childish, but eavesdropping was my best tactic to finding out what was going down in there. I couldn't help myself.

"I'm not interested in another babysitting assignment," I heard Ian say. His tone was less aggressive now. "I don't need to be tethered to a new version of the Italian mob."

"I only kept you tethered to help you, Ian," Director Thatcher told him. She called him by his first name. They had much friendlier relationship when no one else was around. "You have always been an outstanding agent, but after the incident in Thailand, I had to pull you back. It all seemed so personal to you."

"It is personal. I take it personally because no one should be unfazed by the atrocities we see. I'll run my assignments with the same precision Command has come to expect from me, but I won't treat those people like they're just an assignment," he told her in no uncertain terms.

There was a long pause before Thatcher spoke.

"Is she ready?" she asked, redirecting the conversation.

"Yes." Ian's tone was definitive. I was glad to hear it.

"Are you sure?"

Silence.

What's happening? Why isn't he answering?

"What is this?" Ian asked.

"Her computer login reports. She's trying to track Damon Pazzia."

Shit!

"Is this going to be a problem?" Thatcher continued.

"No."

"Good. Because I can't have agents out there on personal missions of vengeance," she said.

"She's been through a lot, and we have to remember that we plucked her from obscurity and dropped her into this life," he said. "She's a good agent and an asset to this division. Victoria still has some things to learn, but that will come as she gains more experience." Ian was likely pissed at me for going behind his back and searching for Damon, so it was kind of him to defend me to Thatcher.

"I'd hate to lose her, Ian, but…"

"She's *ready*," Ian reiterated.

"Are you?"

"What do you mean?"

"Are you ready to treat her like you do everyone else on your team?" Thatcher asked.

"Of course." Ian's tone was strong and defensive. He took issue with being questioned about his ability to lead with objectivity. His interaction with Carter in Padova had made that clear.

"She's had quite an effect on you, hasn't she?" I heard Thatcher say. There was a long pause before Ian replied. I pictured him twisting his bottom lip between his thumb and index finger, as was his habit when he was in contemplation.

"She has. And I'm a better agent for it. But my relationship with Victoria doesn't change my ability to do my job." Ian's answer was short and to the point.

"I believe you believe that, Ian," Thatcher said. "I won't make any changes to your team quite yet. She trusts you, and I think *she'll* be a much better agent because of that. But be aware that I'll be keeping an eye on you both. You are an invaluable member of this division, and I believe Miss Asher will prove to be as well. But I won't compromise the integrity of this department because you decided to fall in love."

Footsteps scuffed on the carpet, and I backed away from the door. Ian must have been right up on it, because I heard him clearly even a few feet away.

"Is there anything else?" Ian asked. A muffled response from Thatcher preceded the click of the doorknob. I scurried to the couch and sat, crossing my legs casually. The door opened and I heard Thatcher speak.

"Be swift, Ian. Once Wren is safe here in London, we can ascertain what she's supposed to lead us to."

Ian appeared from Thatcher's office and I stood, a bright smile plastered across my face.

"Come in, Miss Asher," Thatcher called from her office. My eyes darted between Ian and her open door. He said nothing, but glowered at me as I moved toward the door.

"You wanted to see me?" My heart raced as I entered Thatcher's office and closed the door behind me. She raised a finger at me as she finished composing something at her computer. I took in her office while I waited. It was classically decorated with streamlined, modern furniture and beautiful artwork adorning the walls. I got the feeling she wanted the focal point of the room to be the artwork, which is why all the furniture was gray, black, and white. Each piece that hung on the wall popped.

"Are you a lover of art, Miss Asher?" Thatcher asked, meeting me where I stood admiring the beauty on her walls.

"Yes, but I don't know much about it," I told her. "They're all lovely."

"I personally acquired each piece from the artist directly. I'm the *only* owner. They had never even left their home country before I bought them. They are, as I'm sure you can tell, sources of great pride for me."

"I can see that." I noticed the signature on three of the pieces. "You like this artist a lot, huh?"

"Yes," she answered. "These are by a uniquely talented artist from a small village in Russia called Dovstov. The price I paid for these was enough to take care of his family for decades, maybe even the rest of their lives." My eyes shot up in surprise. "When you consider the currency exchange rate, of course."

"Of course. Well, it must be a wonderful feeling to be the sole owner of something so unique." I wasn't sure where she was going with this. Was it because she had the power to have something no one else could? Or was she just trying to show off?

We stood there in awkward silence. Okay, so I was the only one feeling awkward. She stood there with her perfect, poised posture and waited to see if I was going to say something. For fear that I would stick my foot in my mouth, I endured the silence and waited for her to speak first. A triumphant moment in my book.

"How are you feeling, Victoria? You've been training for three months now. Do you feel prepared for the field?" After her exchange with Ian, I figured I better not complain about the training exercise today. "Yes, ma'am. I've had excellent training and feel as prepared as anyone can until they actually get out there."

"Luckily for you, you've already had some experience in the field."

I didn't know what to make of her comment. I couldn't decide if she was trying to intimidate me, or remind me of how not to do things once I got out there. Either way, I didn't have much of a reply.

"Yes, I suppose so."

"You know, I've been tempted to move you to another team," she said. A rush of electricity rocketed through my nervous system. She didn't have to elaborate. We both knew what she was talking about. Ian and I had been so careful not to display our relationship inside the walls of INTERPOL so there would be no qualms about our commitment to Rogue. But I could see it in her eyes. I knew exactly where she was going. I had my own doubts about my ability to balance this new life of mine and my relationship with Ian, but I wanted to be the one to decide where things went.

"Our relationship isn't an issue." I spoke with confidence to reassure both of us that my job with Rogue was my priority.

"I'm not going to move you to another team, Victoria," Thatcher said.

"But you want us to end things."

"Demanding you end your relationship with Ian would only leave you both distracted. I may run a covert operation with skilled men and women trained to kill, but I'm not heartless, Miss Asher." She raised one corner of her mouth in a kind of smile. "I'm simply asking you to use caution. Ian's training is ingrained in him. Yours has had little time to develop roots. Like any workplace romance, you'll have to find a way operate within both the requirements of your job *and* your feelings for one another. When push comes to shove on an assignment, your objective must be clear, and being an agent must come first."

"I can assure you that we will be completely professional. You have nothing to worry about."

"I'm glad to hear that you're focused." She paused before she brought us back to the assignment before me. "Ian will have the full report for the assignment. Find Wren and have her back here as quickly as possible." Thatcher opened the file that had been quietly sitting at the center of her desk and began looking over whatever was inside.

"Is there anything else I need to know?" I nodded and looked at the file.

"No. These are the logistics for the team I'm sending to Belgium. I'm doing my best to get Jeremy out of there. I don't want to have to tell his daughter that her father is dead. Nor do I want to tell Jeremy that we were not able to get to his daughter in time." She stared at me blankly. It took me a second to realize that was her way of dismissing me.

"Right. I better catch up to Ian." *Get it together, Vic*, I told myself. I cracked my neck once on each side and steeled myself as I headed down the hall to look for Ian. I found him exiting an office with a file in his hand. I plastered that same grin I had on when he left Thatcher's office. It was probably overkill, but I didn't know how to split the difference in the moment.

"How'd it go?" I asked.

"Let's walk."

Each step down the hall filled me with anxiety. I contemplated redirecting our conversation to our mission to find Wren Strasser, but decided to jump in with both feet and address the elephant in the room.

"I had no idea they were monitoring my computer," I began.

Ian came to a sudden halt. "You were eavesdropping?"

"Of course I was eavesdropping. What did you expect?"

Ian sighed and picked up his stride. I hurried along beside him as I had learned to do down the halls of the INTERPOL offices. He stopped again and then looked at me before grabbing my hand and pulling me into a storage closet.

"This is romantic."

"You have to stop looking for him, Victoria. I've already warned you about how distracting your focus on him can be," he said. "Now Thatcher knows, and she's going to be watching you even more closely."

"Sounded like she plans to keep an eye on both of us," I said.

"Yes. She's going to be watching us both. But you belong here now. I won't be spending my time trying to convince you to go anywhere ... not like before. That makes me elated and scared at the same time."

I reached up and touched Ian's cheek. "You've trained me well. With you as my team leader, I can't fail."

"You know that's not true. No matter how well trained you are, things happen, and you have to be ready for anything." Ian said.

"I know. Sometimes I wonder if we should put a pin in us and get me settled into being an agent first," I suggested.

"No," he said sternly. "We're good as long as we can stay focused." He looked at me over his nose disapprovingly.

"By 'we' you mean me," I said. Ian raised his eyebrows expectantly. "Yes, of course! I am laser focused!"

"And you'll stop searching for Damon?" There was only one right answer to give him.

"Yes. I will stop searching for Damon," I said.

Ian gave me a crooked smile before leaning in and kissing me sweetly. "Good girl."

We exited the storage closet and continued our path down the hallway, having only been seen by a janitor who barely gave us a second look. With the things he saw and overheard, two agents coming out of a storage closet was probably the most normal thing he'd see all day.

We turned a corner and then entered a large meeting room.

"Adam! You're home!" I ran to him and threw my arms around his neck and hugged him tightly, almost knocking Claudia out of the way.

"Hey, Vic! Yeah, I got back last night. Ian wanted it to be a surprise." Adam kissed me on the cheek before letting me go.

"Well he's kept me busy enough with training. I don't know when he would have had *time* to tell me."

"I didn't realize you'd be out on assignment so quickly," Adam continued.

"Yeah, I've got my first assignment. It doesn't sound like anything huge, but I'm ready," I told him excitedly.

"I heard about that," Claudia said. "I'm sure you're ready, and no, it doesn't sound like a big deal. Sounds like you two are just going to give this girl a ride from Oxford back here to London."

"It's kind of a babysitting job, but you never know how things are going play out, right?" I said.

"I'll make sure you've got what you need … not that you're going to need much of anything," Adam said. "Claudia and I are headed to Belgium with the secondary team on this assignment."

"Thatcher said she was sending a team to get Jeremy Strasser." Although they'd be far away, I liked knowing that we were working toward the same goal. "I'm glad it's you two."

"We've gotta go meet up with the rest of that team. We're heading out tonight." Adam hugged me and kissed me again on the cheek. "Don't worry. You're going to do great. And this assignment is going to be a piece of cake." I said my goodbyes before Ian pulled Adam aside to go over some logistics for the assignment. He opened the folder he'd been carrying and showed some papers to Adam.

"I'll see you back here in a few days" I said to him. I walked with Claudia as she moved toward the doorway. "Can I talk to you for a minute?" I whispered. We took a few more steps toward the door and out of Ian's earshot.

"What's up? Everything okay?" she asked.

"I just wanted to apologize for earlier," I told her. "I was a brat, and I'm actually pretty embarrassed about how I acted on the roof."

"It's cool. You're still learning, Vic. You gotta give yourself some time. You'll be thinking like an agent before you know it. No one I know is worried about you at all. Carter even asked how kickass you were now that you've had some actual training," she laughed.

"Well, I appreciate it," I smiled. "Listen, um, before you go … can you do something for me?"

"Sure!"

I looked back at Ian, who had his head buried in the Wren Strasser file.

"I need you find Damon."

Chapter 5

It took a lot of convincing, but Claudia finally agreed to do some digging for me. It was a blurred line, but I was technically sticking to my promise to Ian. I wasn't looking for Damon, Claudia was.

Oxford was a little over an hour from London. We put our game faces on and focused on the assignment: finding Wren Strasser and bringing her back to London. I reviewed the small file on Wren from the passenger seat while Ian drove. She was a third year art student at the University of Oxford, and she shared a flat with another girl who was an art student as well. Also included were scans of some of her paintings. She was good. Really good. I wondered if Thatcher knew how good she was, being the art aficionado that she was.

I studied her picture. She was my age with long reddish hair. She had brown eyes, and her only distinguishing mark was a mole next to her left ear. She looked like your average 20-year-old college student.

"She doesn't have a job outside of school." I looked at the clock on the dashboard. "It'll be almost seven before we get there. We'll have to go straight to her flat."

"Very good," Ian commended.

"It's not rocket science, Ian. It's pretty obvious what we should do to find her. And you don't have to stroke my ego." I let out a defeated sigh. I was beginning to agree with Ian that this was nothing but a babysitting assignment. I had been so excited to have my first mission, but the more I thought about it, the more that feeling faded. Not that I was hoping to use one of the guns Adam prepared for us, but truthfully, it was a pretty boring assignment.

"I'm serious, Victoria. This isn't a training exercise, so every observation you make is key."

"I'm trying to see it that way, but this seems like a pretty lame assignment."

"You'd rather be sent on a dangerous mission with car chases and shoot outs?" he asked.

"No," I answered. "I'm just saying that this seems about as exciting as waiting tables at The Clock on a Monday night."

Ian reached over and took my hand. "This is my fault. I was a prat in Thatcher's office. Don't let that determine how you feel about this assignment."

"Did you just use British slang?" I chuckled. I had known Ian for four months and hadn't heard him use any British slang other than a joke about Carter being an arse.

"That I did!" He laughed. "Seriously, though … I really don't want you to feel like this assignment is anything less than important. It's my own issues with Thatcher having made me a mafia babysitter for so long that had me miffed in her office. This is important, Victoria. Wren's life depends on us finding her and bringing her back to London. We treat this like we would any other assignment."

"Of course. You're right. Get the girl. Bring her back to London. Easy is better than perilous." I squeezed Ian's hand and then drew it away so I could rifle through the papers in her file again. "So what are we going to tell her?"

"I find that brief honesty is a good way to start with civilians," Ian replied.

"'*Brief* honesty?' Oh really? I seem to recall the barrel of your gun in my gut when we first met." I smirked and raised an eyebrow.

"I'm never going to live that down, am I?" he asked, mirroring my expression.

"Probably not."

We parked the car about a block from Wren's building. Ian put his hands on his hips and surveyed the area. "This place seemed so much bigger before."

"You've been here?" I asked.

"A long time ago," he answered. "I dated a girl who moved to Oxford the summer before we graduated."

"Oh." Something strange tangled inside my belly. I twisted my mouth as I realized it was jealousy, which was ridiculous.

We walked down the sidewalk in front of buildings that made the American idea of history look pathetic.

"This is it." Ian opened the door to the brick building and put his hand on the small of my back as I walked in before him.

I searched my surroundings and looked for anything that seemed like it might be out of place. It was your typical English building. Brick on the outside with steep, narrow steps that creaked on the inside. We reached the second floor and literally ran into a couple making out against the wall.

"Oh, um … sorry," I stuttered.

"No worries, love," the girl said with a thick British accent. She smiled mischievously. Her boyfriend was too busy kissing her neck and groping her body to notice us. I smiled awkwardly and continued moving down the hall.

Ian chuckled as I regained my composure. "Something funny?" I asked.

"Just thinking about the times Mrs. Dover caught us doing the same thing in the hall outside *your* flat." He gave me a sexy smile and I couldn't keep myself from smiling back at him.

A few steps more and we reached Wren's door. The groping couple relocated and we were left alone as we knocked. There was no answer. I closed my eyes and pressed my ear to the door to listen for movement.

"Anything?" Ian asked.

"I don't hear anything. If anyone's in there, they're quiet as a mouse," I whispered. I stepped back and nudged Ian with me as I watched under the door for shadows. I shook my head.

"We might find her somewhere on Park End Street," Ian answered.

"What's on Park End Street?" I asked.

"Anything there is to do in this part of town happens on Park End. A lot of the bars do student club nights," he answered. "It's not far from here."

"Are you sure it's been a while since you've been here?" I asked suspiciously as we walked down the stairs and outside.

"Yes. It was a *very* long time ago." He rolled his eyes and tugged at my sleeve to keep moving.

"What's the plan if we don't find her?"

"There's a hotel on Park End. We'll set up there if we need to, and then start fresh in the morning. Check her schedule to see where she'll be and when."

Ian drove us to Park End Street where the Royal Oxford Hotel sat perched on the corner. It was eight, and the street was beginning to fill with people. They milled about on the sidewalk, friends connecting for a drink and students meeting up for a study date. I wondered if Wren was out there.

My mind wandered and I contemplated what being a college student would look like for me. Would I blend in? Would I make friends? Would I *last*? I didn't know. And even though I'd only been a Rogue agent for a short time, I didn't know if I'd ever be able to transition back into a normal life. I had already experienced too much for anything ordinary to ever be satisfactory again.

I broke my gaze when Ian put his arm around my waist.

"I thought we agreed we were going to focus on being *agents* in the field," I reminded him.

"We are. We're *agents* posing as a couple on a busy street in Oxford. As I recall, you and Carter did something similar in Padova. Which reminds me, I still owe him for that kiss he planted on you." He smirked.

I snickered. "Whatever you say, *boss*."

I was concerned that acting as we normally did would confuse things for me. I wanted to be sure I could do my job, be in love with Ian, and not let either get in the way of the other. It seemed this was my test. I would never know if I could handle everything until the challenge was in front of me.

We walked through the door of a bar called Kiss, and I scanned the crowd for Wren. Her picture was etched in my mind, and I felt confident I would know her when I saw her. The bar was painted black with white accents and big, red lipstick kisses scattered about on the walls. I was shocked at how many people were already there at eight o'clock. Clubs back home didn't get started until at least ten.

My hand in his, I walked behind Ian as we snaked through the crowd and bellied up to the bar.

"Ian Hale!" A loud, female voice with a strong Eliza Doolittle accent shouted above the noise of the crowd. Ian let go of my hand and threw his attention toward the voice. "I can't believe me eyes! C'mere, you!"

A very blonde woman with fantastically fake breasts perched herself up from behind the bar and reached her arms around Ian's neck. He reciprocated the hug with greater enthusiasm than I was comfortable with.

"Kitty! Oh my God! What are you doing here?" Ian shouted like a frat boy across the bar.

"I run this place! My brother opened it a while back as an investment, and it's been my baby ever since. I haven't seen you since, well, you know!" Kitty winked at Ian knowingly. "That was a pretty hot and heavy night! I thought I'd never see you again! What've you been doing?" Her accent, blonde hair, and low cut v-neck t-shirt were what teenage boys' dreams were made of, and there she was pawing at Ian like she had rights to him.

"I was a Green Beret for a bit and then I got out. I went into the private sector," he explained.

"Yeah … I was sorry to hear about your mum and sister. They were both real sweethearts. I bet you did the funeral up right beautiful," she replied.

"They were cremated, and the service was lovely. Thank you, Kitty."

I suddenly felt like a third wheel and determined to remedy that.

"Hi!" I shouted as I leaned in closer to Ian. "We haven't met!" I extended my hand so she'd have to take hers off of Ian to shake mine.

"Where are my manners? Victoria, this is Kitty Hans. She's an old friend," Ian stuttered. "Kitty, this is my friend, Victoria."

"Well aren't you a doll! She's a doll, Ian!" Kitty declared with a hearty laugh.

"What's your best on tap?" I asked, not responding to her compliment. Ian's head snapped in my direction and he shot me a look. I hated beer.

"I'm a Harp girl myself," she answered.

"Then a Harp it is! My *friend*, Ian, is picking up my tab tonight. Isn't *he* a doll?"

"Sure, love!" Kitty stepped to one side, tilted a glass under the Harp tap, and pulled the long handle.

"Thanks so much!" I shouted over the music as she set the glass now filled with bubbly liquid in front of me. I took a long draw from the glass and smiled. *Performance of the century.* "I'm going to look for our other friend." I pushed away from the bar and weaved my way through the crowd. I looked back once to see Ian watching me, but then Kitty got his attention and I was a second thought.

It's fine. I'm fine. I was there to do my job, and that's what I was going to do. This was my test, right?

I moved through the crowded bar and found myself on the small dance floor. I didn't see Wren anywhere. I drank my beer and shimmied to the other side of the room where there was a seating area. For a minute I let myself forget why I was there. I let myself remember the nights Tiffany and I would hit South Beach and see which club she could get us into by flirting with the bouncer. And for a minute, I let myself wish that was still my much less complicated life.

"You look like you're looking for someone," a clean-cut guy with dark hair and a polo shirt said to me. He grasped my elbow and leaned in close to my ear so he didn't have to yell. When he was done speaking I looked at him. He was cute. The kind of Oxford boy you brought home to meet your parents.

"Is it that obvious?" I said with a flirty laugh.

"You're American?"

"I stick out like a sore thumb, huh?" I smiled and tossed my hair behind my shoulders. "I'm looking for my friend. Maybe you know her? Her name is Wren Strasser."

"Sorry! I don't. But you're welcome to have a seat with me while you keep an eye out for her," he said politely. *So that's how clean-cut guys hit on a girl. Huh. That was kind of nice*, I thought. Maybe one day I'd get a chance to tell Tiffany how the other half live.

"That won't be necessary," Ian said as he took my other elbow in his hand and tugged me away from my suitor. In the process, he took my beer and placed it on a table.

"Whoa, mate!" I heard the guy call as Ian escorted me down a hall and into the single person restroom. It was the cleanest bar bathroom I'd ever been in.

"What are you doing?" I asked furiously.

"I was about to ask you the same thing," he said harshly as he closed and locked the door behind us.

"Well, let's see, while you were playing catch up with Boobs McGee, I was actually looking for Wren." I crossed my arms and waited for his reply.

"Seriously? That's what this is about? You're out there flirting with some guy because you're pissed we ran into my ex-girlfriend from when I was a *teenager*?" He stepped back and looked at me, astonished. "Everything I do in the field is to accomplish the goal set before me. If I had to be single in those moments with Kitty, then that's what I was going to do to get whatever information she may have been able to give me. None of it changes anything about the way I feel about you."

"Why is it okay for you to be single to get information but not me?" I challenged. He didn't answer. "Did you really just assume that I abandoned my mission to flirt with some random guy because I was jealous?" My heart ached with disappointment. "Is that what you really think of me?"

Ian let out a heavy sigh. "No. That's not what I think of you. You're right. I'm sorry. I was foolish. You're a trained agent, and I trust you to do your job. We have to do whatever it takes to complete our mission." He stepped closer to me and reached out his hand. I was too pissed and pushed his hand away. "What else is bothering you?"

I stopped and searched myself while Ian waited for my reply. I didn't like seeing him with Kitty, but as he said, that was part of the job. If I was honest, her pawing him wasn't what really bothered me. "I didn't know your mom and sister had been cremated," I finally said.

"What?" Ian's forehead creased as he drew his eyebrows in.

"You never told me that," I said. "And then you just volunteered that information to Kitty while I stood there feeling like an idiot."

"You never asked," he said quietly.

"I never asked because I didn't think you wanted to talk about that part of your life."

"When did I ever tell you that? I would tell you anything you wanted to know. There is no part of my life that is off limits to you, Victoria. Don't you understand that?" Ian stepped forward as my back hit the wall. He looked at me with determined eyes and entwined our fingers at our sides.

"We can't do this here. Let's just find Wren and go home," I said.

"No. We're going to do this now. In the ladies' bathroom in a bar in Oxford, we're going to do this." Ian softened his expression and caught my eyes. I was entranced. The blaring music faded away, and all that was left was the sound of our rhythmic breathing.

A loud bang on the door echoed in the small bathroom, signaling my reprieve.

"C'mon! Go shag somewhere else!" a girl shouted through the door.

"Bugger off!" Ian shouted back. He looked at me with determined eyes and I couldn't think straight. The door rattled again. Irritated, Ian unlocked the door and pulled it open, revealing the disrupter of our moment.

"'Bout time! There's a hotel down the street, you know," the girl snapped. I caught her eye and realized that our bathroom occupancy couldn't have been more perfectly disturbed. The girl standing before us had the same long auburn hair, brown eyes, and mole next to her left ear that I had studied in the car on the way from London.

"Wren Strasser?" I asked.

"Yeah. Who's askin'?"

Chapter 6

Ian and I looked at each other, shocked that Wren had unknowingly found us. In a split second, we each grabbed one of Wren's arms and dragged her into the bathroom. It wasn't the smoothest move, but it beat stepping outside and stalking her at the bathroom door like a couple of creepers.

"Oh, ay! I'm not into that sort of thing, but I'm sure there's someone out there that is," she protested as we closed and locked the door behind her.

Ian straightened his shirt and ran his fingers through his hair as he refocused on our assignment.

"My name is Ian Hale, and this is Victoria Asher. Your father sent us for you," he told her firmly.

"What do you mean my father sent you?" She narrowed disbelieving eyes at us.

"We don't want to alarm you, but your father is in some trouble. He has concerns that the people who are threatening him, the people he works for, may come after you as leverage against him," I explained. She thought for a moment before she replied.

"That's ridiculous. I saw my father a week ago and he was perfectly fine. And my dad works at a research lab in

Brussels. Seriously, they're all science swots." She crossed her arms and looked at us as if she had caught us in some kind of prank. "So if you'll both leave, I'll get on with my business here."

"Your father, Jeremy Strasser, sent a message to Director Thatcher at INTERPOL, that..." I began.

"Wait. What?" Wren's arms dropped and so did her suspicious expression. "Penny Thatcher?"

"Yes," I replied. "You know who that is?"

"She's an old friend of my dad's. He's talked about her and her husband, Geoffrey before."

"So you know he's in trouble if he's reached out to Thatcher," I said softly. "And you may be, too. We need you to come with us, and we're going to make sure you're safe."

"Okay ... um ... now I *really* have to go, so ... could you ..." she motioned to the door. Ian and I awkwardly opened it and stepped outside. The music was so loud. I was amazed at just how much of the sound the bathroom door muffled.

The door to the bathroom finally opened and Wren appeared, her face pale. "I just tried to call my dad. He didn't answer. And he didn't reply to my text either. He never does that."

"We'll take you to your flat so you can get a few things. Then we'll head back to London, where you'll be safe," Ian told her. He was firm, but not commanding. He had softened since we first met.

"I don't know anyone in London. Where am I supposed to stay?" Wren asked.

"Penny Thatcher is there. She'll make sure you're in the most secure safe house in London," Ian said.

"Okay," Wren replied. Her eyes shifted from left to right as she searched for answers we couldn't give her yet. I wasn't sure exactly how much we should even tell her.

We weaved through the bar crowd, and I spotted the make-out couple from the hall at Wren's flat. The guy was groping the girl again, but this time she eyed me, expressionless. I waited until we got outside to say anything to Ian.

"We need to hurry," I told him. He dipped his chin and waited for my explanation. "The couple that was making out at Wren's … they were in the bar. She gave me this *look*. Something about it..." Ian nodded in agreement.

Ian took the stairs in Wren's building two at a time while she followed and I covered the back. Everything looked clear, no one pretending to make out in the hallway or even hovering around the building at all.

When Wren opened the door, I half expected to see the place completely tossed. It wasn't. Everything looked to be in order, but I wanted to be certain. I held an arm out in front of Ian and Wren as I stepped into the room first. It was a small flat with sparse furniture. The pillows on the sofa were cockeyed, as pillows tend to be, and the drawers to the small buffet by the dining table were all closed, as they should have been.

And then a few details began to jump out at me.

"Have you rearranged your furniture lately?" I asked.

"No," Wren answered. "My flat mate is an obsessive creature of habit. I can't change up where the spoons and forks lie in the drawer without her freaking out."

The dust pattern on the end tables told me the lamps had been moved. They were pushed to the side, revealing a bald, dust-free crescent moon shape. The sofa and chair had been moved as well, revealing the divots in the carpet where they once sat.

"Someone's been here. You need to gather a few things and then we need to go … quickly," I instructed.

We began to move toward Wren's bedroom when a tall, dark-haired, hipster-looking guy stormed through the door. Ian and I instinctively drew our guns and took aim.

"Whoa!" the guy shouted as she raised his arms.

"Stop!" Wren shouted. "This is my boyfriend, Char."

Ian and I lowered and holstered our weapons, both irritated.

"What's he doing here?" Ian asked.

"When you weren't at Kiss, I got worried so I took a taxi and came right over," Char said. Wren flew across the room and into Char's arms and started crying. "What's going on? Who are these people?" He slid his thumb across her cheek, wiping the tears that had fallen.

"These are special agents. It's kind of hard to explain, but my dad is in trouble," Wren began. "He…"

"That's classified information, Mr. …" I interrupted before Wren could say too much.

"Wallace. Charlie Wallace," Char said, filling in the blank.

"You can tell Char anything," Wren offered as she wrapped her arms around his waist.

"I'm sure, but it's still classified," Ian reiterated. "Now, if you'll get your things, we can be on our way."

"It'll be okay, Char," she said as she calmed herself. "Once we stop by your place for you to pack a few things, we'll be on our way … together."

"He's not coming with us." Ian's voice was decisive.

"What? He has to!" Wren protested.

"We were sent to get you and only you. Once we get to London and have a better handle on the situation, we'll set up a secure line for you to communicate with him," Ian told her.

"It'll be okay, baby," Char told her. "If you trust them, then let them do their jobs. I don't want to mess anything up by tagging along. I'm sure everything will be fine, and you'll be home before you know it." Char smiled reassuringly at her, which seemed to calm her. Wren's shoulders dropped from their tense position and she let out a small sigh.

Wren reluctantly left Char's arms and hurried to her room. She came back a few moments later with a backpack slung over her shoulder. Before we left, she wrote a note to her roommate saying an old friend of the family had invited her to London, and that she'd be back in a few days.

Ian agreed to take Char home on our way back to London. He didn't live far, only about ten minutes away. Wren snuggled up with Char in the back seat, already having begun her goodbyes. Ian pulled up to the curb outside Char's building and we let the lovebirds out to have a moment alone under the glow of the streetlight.

"Am I being weird, or is there something unsettling about this Char guy?" I suggested.

"He was pretty agreeable about us whisking Wren away. Maybe he's just not that into her and he's happy for the distraction," Ian suggested with a slight chuckle.

"Ha ha. I'm serious. Doesn't it seem strange that he would rush right over just because Wren wasn't at the bar? And he arrived only a few minutes after we did. When he didn't see her there, wouldn't a 'where are you?' text have been your first approach?"

Before I could explore my reservations with Ian further, the exploding sound of a gun being fired roared around us. I lurched around in my seat while Ian jumped out of the car to find Wren and Char in a huddled pile on the sidewalk.

"Is anyone hurt?" I shouted through the still-open door as I retrieved my gun.

"No, I don't think so," Wren replied before both of them climbed into the back seat and crouched down at Ian's instruction. Shots fired again. "Who is that? Why are they shooting at us?"

"My best guess is it's the people your father warned would come after you." I drew my gun and searched the dark street, trying to determine which direction the shot came from.

"Did you see anyone following us?" Ian demanded. His tone was almost accusatory. It was my job to be aware of those things, and it seemed I had missed something. He didn't look at me, but instead surveyed our surroundings with me. We needed to know where the shots were coming from so we didn't fire back in the wrong direction.

"No. Nothing," I barked. Being followed is an easy observation. Even a few car lengths behind, a car that makes *every* turn that you do stands out. "I *know* we weren't followed." I searched the lighted areas on the street for our attacker, but it wasn't until my eyes adjusted to the shadows that I saw her. She was hidden in the darkness, easily twenty yards away, but I knew it was her. Her eyes were giving me the same cold stare as when I passed by her in the bar.

"Ian," I said. "It's her. The girl from make-out couple."

"If they didn't follow us, how the hell would they know to find us here?" Ian snapped as he threw the car in reverse, the tires smoking as the engine roared.

"That's an excellent question." I rolled the window down and fired three shots at the woman. I missed each time. Hot Lips emptied her magazine at us, hitting the side of the car twice.

"If you could hit and disarm her, that would be lovely!" Ian yelled as he continued to maneuver the car in reverse.

"It's dark!" I shouted. "And why are we moving away from her? Shouldn't we be trying to take her down?" Nothing I shot at her came close enough to make her flinch. When we reached a roundabout, Ian whipped the car around and we sped away, leaving the make-out queen behind us.

"Our mission is to keep Wren safe and get her back to London. We can't go running into a gun fight with a civilian in tow," Ian declared.

"So for much for this being a boring babysitting assignment," I joked. Ian shot me a look that told me he was not amused.

"Maybe they've been following me," Wren offered. "I mean, I've been over here to Char's a lot. Oh my God, I'm so sorry, Char!"

"Shh, shh…" Char sounded as he stroked Wren's hair. She was shaking against his chest, his arms enveloping her. "It's okay, love. I'll have them take me to my mum's and …"

"No!" Wren shouted. "If they followed me here, they may have followed you to your mum's, too. I mean … that's something they might do to get at my dad through me, right?" she speculated. "You're not safe. He has to come with us!" Her directive to Ian did not go over well with him, but he couldn't deny the truth in what she said. We had no guarantees that Char would be safe. Whoever was after Wren could just as easily use Char to get to her. And judging by her reaction, that wouldn't be difficult. If we left him, we'd have a domino effect of one person after another being used as leverage.

"Fine. He can come, but I make no promises for how long he'll be with us."

Ian's nostrils flared as he white-knuckled the steering wheel. He kept his steely eyes on the road until he got Thatcher on the phone fifteen minutes later. Ian didn't want the assignment in the first place, and now we had taken on an additional person in this babysitting job gone awry.

"Is this some kind of safe house, or something?" Char asked as we entered my flat.

"Nope. This is my place," I told him.

Ian had been on the phone with Thatcher for nearly an hour. The safe house building had a gas leak, and all the residents had been evacuated. Informants waiting to testify against some of England's most dangerous criminals currently occupied the other two locations in London. That left Thatcher scrambling to secure another safe house, preferably one far from Oxford.

With no safe house location, our best option was to make our way to the safest place Ian and I knew: our flats. And since we had Char with us, Ian would be forced to play host as well. As soon as Thatcher could give us the location of the safe house, we would take Wren there and then put Char on a train back to Oxford. Until then, this would be our adventure in babysitting.

"Where's my dad?" Wren asked. "Someone is bringing him here, right?"

"Another team is working on that. You were our assignment. Your father was adamant that we keep you safe." I wasn't sure if Wren was comforted at all by my assertion that her father was concerned for her safety. She was clearly freaked out by the whole situation, and rightfully so. "Wren, your father said you would have some information for us." I didn't want to say too much. My gut still didn't trust Char, who was nearly glued to Wren's side. But we didn't have time to waste either. Whatever information we could get for Thatcher would get us closer to saving Wren's father, too.

Wren furrowed her brow. "I don't know what it could be."

"Well ... tell me about last time you saw your dad," I said. "Maybe there's a detail that you didn't think anything of at the time."

"Okay. Um ... it was a week ago. He made a surprise visit to see me."

"Did he say anything that made you think he was in trouble?" Char asked. He put his arm around her and rubbed her shoulder. If it wouldn't have clued him into my suspicion, I would have narrowed my eyes and told him to button it, and to let me ask the questions.

"Nothing. It was a really great visit. We went and got tattoos." She chuckled. "It was totally normal!" I'd never heard a daughter explain how getting tattoos was "totally normal" father-daughter bonding. "It's back here." Wren lifted her long hair to reveal a beautiful tattoo of a butterfly. It was yellow with black outlining the wings, and a black design scrolling along the tops of each wing. I'd always been fascinated by tattoos but never brave enough to get one myself. The whole needle-poking-into-my-skin-at-a-rapid-pace thing was kind of a deterrent.

"Do you mind?" I asked Wren as I stepped forward with an extended hand to examine the artwork on her neck.

"Not at all," she smiled. "I know it's totally cliché, a butterfly and all, but at least it's not on my lower back, right?" Wren laughed as Char looked over my shoulder while I stared at the intricate design. My eyes followed the scrolling lines of the design in awe, taking in every detail.

"It's beautiful. What do the numbers mean?" I asked.

"What numbers?" Wren asked, her voice displaying her surprise.

"There are three numbers on each wing," I told her. "Five, four, and nine." I pulled out my cell phone and took a picture to show her.

She chuckled. "I didn't know they were there. That would be my dad's doing. We went to a guy he knew outside of Oxford. Dad said he was an expert at details and since I wanted a butterfly, I had to have a guy who wouldn't scrimp."

"So … what do the numbers mean?" Char reiterated my question.

Button it!

"Oh, right. That was our fake address in Bruges: 945 Bell Tower Terrace."

"I'm sorry. Your *fake* address?" I couldn't hide the puzzled look on my face.

"Dad got us a little getaway place in Bruges just a few blocks from the bell tower. The flat there was small, but my mum left when I was little so it was just the two of us and we didn't need a lot of space. We would spend our time walking the city. It's a lot like Venice with canals and cafés right there by the water. But one of my favorite places was the bell tower at the church. We would sit outside at a café in the square and make up stories about what life would be like to live in the church. One day we gave it an address and started calling it home."

"That sounds really lovely," I said, thinking of my own father and the special moments we shared. I wondered why Wren's mother left them and couldn't think of a single reason why a mother would willingly leave her own child.

"Yeah. When I got a little older, around twelve, we would leave notes for each other in the bell tower behind a loose stone. He always said it would be our special place." She stopped and smiled, enjoying a memory.

"That's amazing, Wren," Char said sweetly. "You never told me about that place."

"I haven't been there in a long time ... haven't really thought about it until now," she said. Char smiled at Wren while I tried to read what was behind his eyes. He caught me watching him as he wrapped his arms around her and seemed to make a show of squeezing her tightly.

"So what information was she supposed to have for you?" Char asked me.

"I'm not sure exactly," I lied. "But perhaps after a good night's sleep it will become clearer in the morning."

I got the two of them comfortable on the couch and offered some tea while we waited for Ian, who was *still* on the phone with Thatcher trying to secure a safe house for us. I also told them about the Chinese place a few blocks down that delivered until two in the morning, and they seemed to be interested. We were all hungry, and I was certain Ian would be up for some cashew chicken.

Ian finally walked through the door. He was less on edge than when we arrived, which was good.

"Looks like I'll have a roommate tonight," he said as he met me in the kitchen.

"They couldn't find another safe house anywhere?" I asked. "Doesn't that seem odd to you?"

"It's unusual, but not unheard of," he answered.

"Well, one night with a house guest doesn't seem so bad," I offered.

"That wasn't part of the plan," he countered.

"Well, sometimes the plan changes, and you have to be flexible, right?"

Ian gave me a crooked smile.

"Just agree with me," I said as we joined Wren and Char in the living room.

"I agree," Wren said.

"Wait, what are we agreeing on?" Ian asked.

"Char thinks we should go to my father in Brussels instead of the safe house. He needs me," she said.

"Absolutely not," Ian barked. "Our orders are to keep you safe, and taking you to the center of the danger is not part of that plan. If it were safe where you father is, he would have asked us to take you there."

Wren's head dropped. "Yes, of course. That makes perfect sense."

Char narrowed his eyes at Ian, causing my gut to do flips. I was glad he'd be staying under Ian's watchful eyes.

"Here's the plan," Ian began after a cleansing breath. "There was a problem with the safe house you were assigned to, so that means you two will be staying with us. Wren, you're here with Victoria, and Char—" Ian let out a defeated sigh. "You're with me."

"Wait. What? We can't stay together?" Char protested.

"No." Ian's face was flat. He was nothing if not old fashioned.

"Honestly, there's not enough room in either of our flats for two guests," I explained.

"It's okay, Char. I'm exhausted, so I'm going to go to sleep." Wren patted Char's leg sweetly.

"Fine. Where do *you* live? Is it far from here? I don't want to be too far from Wren," Char demanded. His tone was sharp, not helping my already skeptical view of him.

"Upstairs, actually," Ian told him. Char acquiesced.

"Great," I said with a smile, hoping to cut some of the tension in the room. "Now that that's settled … I'm famished. Anyone else interested in some cashew chicken?"

Chapter 7

We spent all night trying to keep Wren as calm as possible. From fear to worry to her reminiscing about her father, Wren's emotions were all over the place. It was understandable. I remember the hours when the details of my parents' plane crash were sketchy and no one knew anything. It was agony. I spent the hours of waiting talking with Tiffany because my brother Gil's coping mechanism was to shut down.

Wren told us going to Oxford and her passion for art were all because of her dad. When she lived in Brussels with him, he would take her to Grand Place and teach her about the history there, and they frequently took the train into Paris, where he took her the Louvre and the Arc de Triomphe.

"That's when I fell in love with all forms of art," she said.

By the time I convinced Ian that he had to actually go back to his flat and take Char with him, it was almost one in the morning. We'd had quite a night and were all in need of a good sleep. And I was certain Ian would be knocking at my door no later than eight o'clock, dressed and ready to dispose of Wren, and especially Char.

"Just a few more hours and this babysitting job is over," I reminded Ian quietly as I walked him to my door. Wren was saying her goodnights to Char in the living room.

"Thank God," he smiled. "Outside of being shot at, this has gone remarkably well."

"That's right! You upgraded this mission, didn't you?" I smiled. "I did hear your record for being shot at is twelve minutes. We were hours into this one before the first shot." I chuckled before I looked over my shoulder to make sure Wren and Char will still occupied with each other. "But … I still can't put my finger on the deal with Char."

"Besides showing up ridiculously quickly to her flat, there hasn't been anything that seemed off to me," Ian replied. "But I'm not the one with wicked intuition."

I pressed my lips together as I searched the "wicked intuition" Ian had come to trust and rely on. The evidence was mounting. His interest in the bell tower, the way he looked at me when comforting Wren, and of course, the amount of churning my gut had done since I laid eyes on him. The problem was, the make-out couple was throwing me off. The woman who shot at us tonight was clearly after Wren. So what was Char's deal?

"Yeah … I guess. Could just be that my j-dar is going off," I suggested.

"J-dar?" Ian questioned.

I laughed. "It's something Tiffany and I came up with whenever we were out. She had this way of finding the biggest jerk in the whole place. She was oblivious, but I could read them from a mile away."

"Handy!" Ian chortled.

"It was only handy if Tiffany actually listened to me." I rolled my eyes as I remembered the arguments she would make for why a guy wasn't *that* big of a jerk. Then my heart sank remembering the tears that would roll down Tiff's face after said jerk broke her heart.

We watched Wren lean into Char in the living room. The two held each other in desperation.

Ian took my hand and brought it to his lips. He stepped closer and put his hand on my hip, and I rested my head on his chest and let him hold me.

"I know." Ian's voice soothed me, and I felt like we were going to be okay.

Wren and Char approached and interrupted our moment. I lifted my head and took a step back. We had our personal moment. It was time to be agents Asher and Hale again.

"All set?" Ian asked.

"I guess so," Wren said, drowning us with her disappointed tone that Char couldn't stay with her.

"It'll be fine, love," Char reassured her. "Like you said: we're all tired. Everything will seem better in the morning." He kissed her quickly and stepped through the open door into the hallway. Wren turned back into the living room, flopped onto the couch, and pouted.

"I'll be by around eight." Ian leaned in and gave me a chaste kiss on the cheek. He was painstakingly aware that we were not alone; otherwise, he would have wrapped one arm around my waist and cupped the nape of my neck with his other hand, giving me a passionately romantic kiss as he had done every other time he left my apartment.

I gave Ian a soft smile. "I'll see you then."

Closing the door behind Ian, I heard Wren quietly sobbing in the living room. I made a cup of decaffeinated tea and set it in front of her on the coffee table before I took a deep breath and sat next to her on the couch.

"You doing okay?" I asked absurdly. She was obviously not doing okay, but I didn't know where else to start. She wiped her face and took the teacup in her hands.

"I'll be fine."

"Yes, you will. No one could ever be prepared for a situation like this. You're worried about your dad, and I'm sure having Char around takes some of that stress off." Being with Ian had made me feel better after Gil died. "You'll see him in the morning." I didn't tell her that once we got word on the safe house, she'd have to say goodbye to Char again.

She nodded weakly as she took a sip of tea.

"You two have been together a while?" I asked, making small talk.

"Almost four weeks." A wide grin spread across her face.

"Wait. What? Did you say four *weeks*?" I couldn't have heard her clearly.

"Yes, almost!"

"No offense, but you seem pretty attached to a guy you *just* met." I got the whole instant attraction thing. I had it with Ian. But Wren was acting like she and Char had been together forever and the idea of being apart was unfathomable to her.

"Clearly you've never been in love." She narrowed her eyes at me. "And we didn't *just* meet. We met and it was…" She sighed. "It was everything I ever dreamed finding *the one* would be like."

"Really." I didn't even try to hide my skepticism.

"Yes, really," she said, no longer crying but determined to make her point. "Haven't you ever looked into the eyes of someone, and you knew your life would never be the same? Haven't you ever been with someone, and just the idea of being apart from him made you sadder than you ever thought possible? Haven't you ever been kissed so hard that it blew away every idea you had of what it meant to be really and truly kissed?" She paused for a moment to soften her tone. "It may have only been a few weeks, but when you know … you just know."

I stood up, feeling challenged by Wren's naïve yet accurate insight. I felt all those things with Ian. I remembered the first time he kissed me, and just the thought made me weak in the knees.

"You're right. I'm sorry. I shouldn't have been so judgey." I apologized, but my uneasiness about Char didn't go away. Maybe that was my issue, and not the fact that I had leftovers in my fridge older than their relationship. I was sure a good night's sleep would help clear my head. Plus, we'd get Wren to the safe house in the morning and send Char packing, and then he'd be out of the current equation for good.

"It's okay. A lot of people have a hard time with love-at-first-sight. They call it *insta-love* and say it isn't real, but that's only because they've never experienced it." Wren smiled confidently.

I nodded and changed the subject. "You said you started your adventures in Bruges with your dad after your mom left. Do you mind telling me about that?" This detail from her past had been gnawing at me since she mentioned it so flippantly in the story of the numbers in her tattoo.

"There's not much to tell. I never knew my mum. She was a researcher like Dad, but British. That's how they met. They never married, and I was a baby when she left. Dad never said much about her when I was little, but as I got older and asked, all he would tell me was that my mother was not a good person and that her leaving was the best thing she ever did for us. He would never elaborate," she explained. I could see by her lack of emotion that she had come to terms with this a long time ago. That made me sad for her.

"Why do you think your dad stayed in Belgium? Why not go back to the States?" I was curious why an American soldier wouldn't go home after he was discharged.

"There are two things my father loves most in the world: me, and science." She smiled at the mention of her father's love. "He was courted by a company before he got out of the Army with an offer he couldn't refuse. Don't ask me what he was researching. He's tried explaining his projects to me before, but my right-brained way of thinking just glazes over with confusion. When that job was done, he moved on to another place that was in desperate need of his skills. And then he's been with this lab for a little more than two years now." Tears welled up in Wren's eyes, bringing us full circle to her fears and concerns for her father. "He talked about going back to America, though. I think he was finally beginning to miss it."

"Well," I began. "I'm sure everything is going to be fine. We'll get you to the safe house tomorrow, and then we can talk more about the information your dad said you're supposed to lead us to." Wren gave me a sad smile. "We should hit the hay. I don't know if Char is a morning person, but Ian is going to have his butt down here and ready to go by eight," I chuckled.

"Oh, that won't be a problem. He's a runner. He gets up at five every morning and runs before class," she said.

"Perfect, then. Let me show you to your room. It's small, but then again, everything is small here. I'm still getting used to it." I grabbed Wren's bag and motioned for her to follow me down the short hall. There were no pictures on the wall, or any other decorations to mention in the whole flat actually, just a few knick-knacks I'd picked up at some of the street markets around London but nothing that would necessarily identify this as my home. Ian's place was the same.

"You're American, right?" she asked.

"Yep."

"Did you come to London to be an agent?"

"Uh…" I replied, biting my lip.

"Or is all that hush, hush and top secret?" she replied with an inquisitive smile.

I hesitated for a moment. I hadn't been asked by anyone what brought me overseas. I was always with Ian when out in the city, so the assumption of anyone we spoke to was likely that love brought me here. It may not have been what brought me, but it's what kept me here.

"I came to help a friend. It didn't work out as we hoped. When it was over, I stayed." My answer was short and to the point. No mention of Gil's name or the fact that he was dead. No real details and no tears.

"Oh. I'm sorry it didn't work out. I had a feeling you understood what I'm going through." Wren's tone turned sympathetic and she didn't even know the whole story. I couldn't imagine her response if she did. Either way, I didn't want her sympathy.

"I suppose I do." I stopped in front of the door to the guest bedroom. "Here we are. The loo is there across the hall. Do you want to shower now or in the morning? I can do either, so it's up to you."

"Oh, it's lovely," she said, noting the white, single sleigh bed in the middle of the room. "I'll shower in the morning."

"Sounds good."

"Thank you, Victoria. I know I put up a bit of a fight earlier about Char. I'm just scared. But I'm sure Penny is going to make sure he's okay. I mean … she's a friend of Dad's, so I know I can trust her."

"You can." I patted the doorframe after we said our goodnights and made my way to the loo. After a hot, steaming shower, I crawled beneath the covers of my bed.

It had been a whirlwind day, and my body was thankful for the rest. But despite my exhaustion, I couldn't shut my brain off. I lay there with my eyes wide open, considering Ian. We were smack dab in the middle of an assignment, and I was consumed with thoughts of him. Yes, I was lying in the comfort of my own bed, but my thoughts should have been focused on our mission. Would I be able to continue in the field and keep my feelings under control? I didn't know, and that scared me.

I woke to the sounds of Wren moving around the apartment. Heavy footsteps preceded the small squeak the door to the loo let out just before it latched closed. It was still dark outside, but I wasn't one to judge other girls for how long it took them to get ready. When I wanted to look really good, I could take a good hour and a half to primp. Working at The Clock diner, living in the 'hood, and dating Chad, that didn't happen all that often. But since I'd been with Ian, I had to admit that I'd kept him waiting a time or two.

She is so damn loud, I thought as I lay awake at a quarter of six. I let it go and rolled myself into a blanket burrito as my still-heavy eyes closed. I wasn't able to go back to sleep, but at least I could still get some rest while I considered the day ahead. By sunrise, Thatcher would hopefully have a safe house for Wren, and by the afternoon, I'd be back at INTERPOL being giving a new assignment or being challenged by Ian in a training exercise.

I thought about the information Wren gave me yesterday. The stories of her tattoo and the numbers, and their time in Bruges at the Bell Tower were lovely, but it all seemed too easy. She had no idea what her father was talking about, yet Strasser was adamant that Wren would lead us to this antidote. Would he really have left this all-important cure somewhere anyone could find it?

A loud knock on the door to my flat came about an hour later. I unrolled myself from my coziness and zombie shuffled to the door. The knock came again, a little louder this time. I opened the door to find a harried Ian tapping an impatient foot.

"Where's Char?" he demanded as he stormed in.

"Good morning to you, too, sunshine," I said as I rubbed my sleepy eyes.

"Good morning. Is Char here?"

"If he's not with you, Wren said he runs every morning. He's probably out for a run," I told him through a yawn.

"He said nothing to me about going for a run." Ian scurried into my flat and paced as he swiped at his phone.

"You mean you two didn't stay up all night braiding each other's hair and practicing kissing into a pillow?" I snickered.

"You're not as funny as you think you are, you know." Ian narrowed his eyes at me before softening them. "You really think he went for a run?"

I thought for a minute. "No."

"Any chance he saw just how in-the-way he was and took off?"

"That's a toss up," I answered. "Wren has been up for a while. She's loud as hell, and you know how I can be about my mornings." Ian laughed knowingly with wide eyes. "Let me get the kettle on and a cup of tea going. It's going to kill her if he's taken off without saying goodbye. I need a minute before I break the news to her."

Ian sat at my little table for two while I filled my electric kettle in the sink. Still sleepy, I shuffled from one side of the kitchen to the other as I gathered the tin of loose tea and two cups for us. In a normal world where our lives were not challenged by crazy people with delusions of world domination, I could send my boyfriend off to work every day and feel pretty secure in the fact that he was going to be around for dinner. For that matter, I could feel pretty secure that *I* was going to make it home for dinner, too.

But that was not our world.

"What time is Thatcher expecting us?" I asked.

"I told her we'd have Wren there by nine," Ian answered.

"Oh, great. We have plenty of time. What did she say about Char?" I raised a curious eyebrow.

"I didn't tell her. I'm going to let her enjoy that nugget of a surprise just like we did." He chuckled.

"Any word on the safe house?"

"No and, honestly, she might be better off staying with Thatcher. This whole assignment is personal for her. Seems like keeping Wren close might be best."

After tea and a quick piece of toast, I left Ian in the kitchen and walked back to my bedroom. The bathroom door was open, but the light was off. I looked ahead to the guest room door and saw that it was ajar. My gut started churning, which was a good sign that the "wicked intuition" Ian had come to trust was working. It was also a bad sign because it meant that our day was about to get a lot more complicated.

I knocked lightly on the guest room door.

"Wren?" I called softly. She didn't answer, so I pushed the door open and poked my head in. *Oh, no.* "Ian!"

"What is it?" Ian called as he shot out of the kitchen.

"She's gone," I told him.

"What?" he flew from the kitchen and moved into the empty room, turning around as if he was going to magically summon her. "What would make her leave?"

"Not what. Who. When I left her last night, she felt good about Thatcher helping her and her dad. The only reason she would jump ship is if Char convinced her to."

Ian pulled out his phone and paced the room. "But she was already on board with letting Thatcher help."

"The things we do for love."

I shook my head, trying to fit all the pieces together in my head while Ian called Command. It wasn't just her being rudely loud this morning. "Char got her to let him in. He could have easily texted her, which wouldn't have woken me up. Once she let him in and they were alone, he convinced her to go to Belgium, to go to her father."

"I'll get the location of Strasser's lab in Brussels," Ian began.

"Wait," I said flatly. I didn't know what angle Char was playing, but he was about to deliver Wren into the hands of the people we were trying to save her from. "Have Adam's team keep an eye out for Char and Wren at the lab, but we won't be going there."

"We have to follow the asset, Victoria," Ian admonished. "Wren is our assignment."

"Strasser said Wren would lead us to the cure. She might not know where it is, but I do."

"Where do you think it is?" Ian looked at me with wide eyes full of anticipation.

Now I was the one pacing the floor. It was so obvious, but was it too obvious? "It would have be in a place that would mean something to Wren, a place she would eventually think to go. The bell tower in Bruges."

"The bell tower?"

"You were still on the phone with Thatcher last night when I asked Wren when she last saw her dad. He surprised her a week ago and they went and got tattoos." Ian raised an eyebrow. "Yeah, that's what I thought, too. Anyway ... she showed me and Char this gorgeous butterfly tattoo on the back of her neck. There were numbers hidden in the wings that she didn't know were there: nine, four, and five. She told us that after her mom left, she and her dad used to visit the bell tower in Bruges and eventually created this fantasy that it was their home, and that was the address they gave it. They used to leave notes for each other there. So, I'm thinking that—feeling confident these guys are going to kill him—maybe he left one last note there for her, knowing she'd go there after he was gone. Who knows? He may have even hidden the antidote there, too."

"Do you think he's taking her to the bell tower now." Ian said.

"That depends."

"On what?"

"On whose side Char is really on."

Chapter 8

The regular flight from London to Brussels is just over an hour. The flight from London to Brussels on the INTERPOL jet is 30 minutes. As soon as I explained to Ian why we needed to get to Bruges, he was on the phone with Thatcher explaining the situation. To say she wasn't happy about us losing Wren was an understatement, but Thatcher trusted Ian and arranged for us to take one of INTERPOL's private jets to Belgium.

Ian ended his call with someone at INTERPOL and leaned back calmly in the cream-colored leather seat of the jet. The solitary flight attendant had just served us two very strong cups of black coffee, for which I was grateful. It was going to be a long day, and that lovely cup of English tea was not going to cut it for what was sure to lie ahead.

"So?" My brows reached my hairline as I waited for Ian to brief me on his call.

"Adam and Claudia's team is on alert. They're already watching the lab. If Char takes her there, they'll know," he said. "Do you think she's in danger with him?"

"Honestly?" I sighed. "I don't know. It doesn't make sense that he'd be working for Strasser's boss, not after having been shot at by someone else last night. But if he is, then, yeah, she's in real danger. If he strong-armed her into the back of a car this morning, then I'm thinking he's taking her straight to the lab where they can use her to motivate Strasser to tell them where the cure is," I said.

Ian looked at me with a confident stare. "Do you believe Char is working for Strasser's boss?" He did this sometimes when I was training. He wanted me to stop questioning myself and just make a call. He would tell me that, right or wrong, you just have to make the call. Time is wasted when you waver.

"I am more confident that he is, than that he's not. They've only been dating about month, so the timing would work if Strasser's boss were on to him. But the shootout with Hot Lips last night is throwing me off. If he was hired to find Wren, why send her, too?" This was the best answer I could give him. I was still afraid to say for sure. I just kept thinking that Char could simply be a jerk.

"Then that's how we'll operate. If he turns out to be Prince Charming, I'd rather owe him an apology than Strasser." Ian took a sip of his coffee and looked out the window.

"Why would they even want the cure? Seems to me they'd be happy for it to disappear," I mused.

"Well, the cure in the *right* hands would mean the end of their operation," Ian explained. "They're obviously planning on releasing this virus somewhere. If, say, the World Health Organization had the cure, whatever they plan on accomplishing would be void."

"I don't think I'll ever wrap my brain around the jacked up people of this world." I shook my head.

"I hope you don't."

The jet landed around ten o'clock at a private airstrip just outside Bruges. We deplaned and found a car waiting for us. A black sports car, the kind that is both inconspicuous and a glaring sign that you're part of some kind of undercover agency. Sometimes I think we'd be less obvious in a neon pink Fiat.

I spent the ride into Bruges obsessed with the numbers nine, four, and five. They had to mean something. Strasser was a man of science. I couldn't see him assigning numbers to the bell tower arbitrarily. Fifth floor or ninth? Are there nine floors in the tower? Fourth bell maybe? There was a pattern, and I was going to find it.

Like everything else on this side of the ocean, the buildings in Bruges were ancient, and half of them looked like castles. At the center of the city was a huge square with shops, and cafés with umbrellaed tables outside. The impatient clop of hooves sounded on the cobblestone as horse and carriages waited for tourists. It was so sweet and quaint that I half expected a group of villagers to greet us with baskets of freshly picked vegetables.

"I'm never going to have time to really take in the sights again, am I?" I said to Ian as we crossed through the square. Part of me wanted to slow my gait and stroll through the shops, discovering the treasures that Bruges had to offer, but I had to remember that I put that part of me away when I joined the Rogue division.

"Don't hold your breath. And the desire fades. Eventually it won't even occur to you. But once in a while your team leader might feel generous and give you a month off." He winked. "If that ever happens, you should absolutely take advantage of it and see as much of Europe as you can. Oh, wait…"

"All right, all right!" I chuckled. I rolled my eyes as we crossed the square and found our way to the front of the line to get into the belfry. I couldn't believe there was already a line. I guessed the thing had some real history. It wasn't immune to the modernization of the twenty-first century, though. Inside there was a security checkpoint and Plexiglas protecting the woman Ian was talking to behind the desk.

Ian flashed his credentials as he spoke to the woman, then he turned and nodded, and we began the ascent to the top of the Belfry of Bruges.

We passed through a doorway with an oversized, solid wood door. The stone steps curved around with a doorway leading off the path to the first floor. A few people milled around, taking in the view of the town square from the window and reading the placards with interesting facts about the tower. I surveyed the room, hoping something would jump out at me. I searched for anything that looked like it might be a representation of the numbers, but there was nothing.

We left the room the same way we came in and continued up the steps. The next room was a bust as well, so we crossed through it and found another stairwell leading up. As we climbed, it seemed that there were three levels. Three, which was *not* one of the numbers.

The new millennium had reached the top of the bell tower as well. More Plexiglas filled in the spaces between the old wooden beams that framed the bell. *The* bell. One. My chances of finding the pattern of the numbers were quickly fading.

"I'm sorry, Ian. I'm not seeing anything. There are too many people moving around and too many places for me to look. I can't see anything. Plus, so far there hasn't been anything that remotely appears to connect to the numbers. There's only one bell, and three levels." With my hands on my hips, I blew out a hard breath. We had just gotten there, and I already felt defeated. "Maybe I was wrong."

"It's okay, Victoria. They're clearing the tower now, so you should be able to focus better soon. And there are two more levels to the tower. One bell is here, but there's a huge cylinder on the next level and another bell at the top," he explained.

"That gives me four and five but ... wait ... that wouldn't work. If they left messages for each other, you'd think it would be in one spot. This place is too big to leave them randomly." I paced the room for a few seconds as I gathered my thoughts. "If I were going to leave messages for my twelve-year-old kid, where would I do that? It couldn't be too high, or she wouldn't be able to reach it." The wheels in my head turned like the gears of that bell tower as I wore a hole in the floor.

"Excuse me," a woman said. I raised my head and saw the woman Ian had spoken to earlier standing in the doorway. "We've cleared the tower. Do you know how long you're going to be?"

Ian looked at his watch. "It's eleven fifteen now. Give us until noon. Will that be enough time, Victoria?" he asked.

"Sure. If I haven't figured it out in forty five minutes, you might have to fire me," I scoffed nervously as I turned my attention to one of the windows. I approached it and saw that I had a clear view of the entire square. I watched some people move about and others enjoying a cup of espresso at an outdoor table at the café.

You've only got forty five minutes, Vic, I reminded myself.

The proverbial light went off in my head, and the pieces of the puzzle finally started to fit.

Nine, four, five. Nine forty-five. It's a clock!

"Ian! Is there anything like a clock up here? I mean, outside of the bell going off every hour. Is there anything that represents a clock?"

I shuffled around the room, my eyes darting from the top of walls to the whole scope of the floor, searching for some kind of clock face. Nothing. The area itself was huge, but the actual walkable space was small due to the framing of the bell and the Plexiglas partitions cutting the room in half. I ran up the steps to the fourth and fifth levels, but they were just as small, if not smaller. And I assumed that a parent wouldn't leave notes for his kid on the highest level of a bell tower. It seemed more reasonable to me that their special place would be a little less cramped.

I passed Ian on my way back down and stopped in the second level room. Ian did a one-eighty and immediately followed me. This room was much larger. There were two sets of red doors with small windows in them at either end, and a display of historical information spread out on long tables. It was, as I'm sure it was intended to be, like a museum.

One of the sets of red doors had a huge, round window above it. *That's a clock*, I thought. But it was obviously too high. I shook my head as I lowered it and noticed the ginormous circle on the floor where the sun shone through the window.

"Is this it?" Ian asked, scoping out the sunlight on the floor.

I thought for a minute. "Facing the window or with your back to it, there are only two places that could logically be nine forty-five, and there's nothing there. The floor is concrete, and there don't seem to be any loose stones. No, it's somewhere else."

I walked to the sides of the room, thinking maybe the time wasn't on the floor but represented on the walls. I found nothing. I was rushing myself. I needed to take my time and think. I had to put myself in Strasser's mindset, just like I had with my brother and his journaling strategy. Strasser was a scientist. He didn't do things randomly. This was his daughter, and he would make it fun and logical and easy for her. She was twelve when they started leaving notes. What would all those things look like to a 12 year old?

I moved to the other set of red doors that looked out onto the main square. There were grates over the small windows, but I could still see the scene below. People mingled and took pictures. Tourists went in and out of the shops and sat at the cafés, eating and laughing. It was lovely and picturesque. The scene belonged on a post card, and probably was.

"Are those are the only two cafés in the square?" I pointed to the left where there were awnings and tables with umbrellas.

"No. There are a few," Ian answered and pointed to the other side of the square where the cafés appeared to be closed. Maybe they were only open for dinner?

That made my theory a little more complicated, but not impossible. "What if … what if this door, this window, was the clock? Those cafés sit at the nine forty-five place in the window." I looked at Ian, feeling more sure of myself as a Rogue agent than I ever had. "If they left notes here, they would've seen each other either from the café or from the window." I could just see a young Wren finding the note and then waving excitedly to her father, who sat watching from the café below. Although, after a thought, I wasn't sure that the person in the window could be seen very clearly by the one below. Still, it was a nice image.

Ian nodded and began feeling around the window in the door and then along the bricks framing the doors. He pulled and pushed on them for a good minute before one loosened and he was able to pull it free. I crossed my fingers that we hadn't just broken a piece of ancient history for no reason, but Ian's eyes lit up when he peered in the dark space, and I knew we had found it.

Ian pulled out a small blue box only slightly dirtied from having lived behind a brick. I took the small box in my hand and silently prayed there was a flash drive inside that would reveal everything we needed to know. To our dismay, removing the lid to the box revealed an oddly shaped key and a Post-It note with a cryptic message.

"*Everything you need to know is in the treasure chest*," I read. "What the hell does that mean?"

Ian picked up the key and turned it over in his hand. "By the shape of the key and the number engraved in it, I'm guessing it's a safe deposit box." Ian ran his thumb over the number forty-five that was neatly etched into the head of the key.

"Great. Because there aren't hundreds of locations across Belgium where *that* could be." Defeated, I shook my head.

"Don't limit yourself, darling. It's not uncommon for Europeans to have accounts of all types in different countries," Ian said, examining the key.

"Are you kidding me right now? So this safe deposit box could literally be anywhere? And we don't have eyes on the one person who can lead us to it!"

"Rule number two of being a Rogue agent: roll with it. Nothing is as easy as we hope it's going to be," Ian said.

"*That's* rule number two?" I smirked.

Ian looked at me over his nose and raised an eyebrow at me.

"What's rule number one?" I smiled with sugary sweetness.

"Don't die."

"I like that rule."

"That's why it's number one." Ian put the key back in the box and slid it into his pocket.

"So now what?" I asked.

"We'll head to the safe house in Brussels and see if the other team has eyes on Wren yet," he said.

"Okay," I sighed, feeling like we were barely past square one.

"Hey ... you did really well today. Extraordinary, actually. I'm in awe of how your mind works," Ian said reassuringly.

"It took me too long to figure it out," I complained.

"Bloody hell, woman! You had three numbers and a seven-hundred-and-seventy-four-year-old bell tower to search. Just accept the fact that not only are you good at your job, but you can do what I've never seen anyone do." Ian's chastisement blew out of him in a flurry of frustration.

"Okay, okay. I'm sorry. I just really want to be useful. I don't want to hold up our progress. It's important."

"You'll never hold anything up as long as you're doing your best." Ian's tone and demeanor had calmed.

"All right. I'll try not to be so hard on myself," I agreed.

"Good."

"So, uh ... you just went totally all British on me there," I teased. "That's twice in two days."

"Yes, and don't make me do it again."

"I don't know. I kind of liked it." I smirked. Ian mirrored my expression, and we made our way down the steps just as the ticket lady was on her way up. I hadn't watched the time, but I guessed we were about to overstay our welcome. She and Ian nodded at each other before she turned around and found her place back at the counter.

"What did you say to her to clear the building?"

"I showed her my INTERPOL badge and told her we had official business here." Ian put his hand on the small of my back as he walked next to me and out into the fresh air in.

"Oooh. Badges. Sexy," I joked. "So how does one obtain one of these magical badges that makes anyone do what you tell them?" The warmth of the sun soothed my skin.

"You mean all I've had to do this whole time was flash my badge and you'd do whatever I said? If I had only known!" He laughed. I elbowed Ian playfully in the ribs. "Well ... this isn't common knowledge, but Thatcher just raised my clearance level."

"Oh really?"

"It's all part of her plan," he smiled softly. "She's after an executive position within INTERPOL and wants me to take her place as director of Rogue if she gets it."

I stopped in my tracks. "You would leave the field?"

"I don't have to. I ... I wanted the position before, but now..." Ian looked at me with soft eyes. "It's something we need to talk about."

"Ian, it's okay," I said reassuringly. I truly wanted what was best for Ian and his career. No matter what he decided, we'd figure it out, but it was still a blow. I had just gotten into the field, and Ian was considering leaving it.

"So where's the safe house? Far?" I asked as we began walking again.

"Not far. It's about half way between Brussels and here. You'll like it. It'll remind you of the factory outside Bologna."

"That does *not* excite me," I sneered. That first safe house was the place where Ian and Adam trained me like a dog. It was also the place where Ian and I were ambushed and I woke to find him beaten and strung up from the rafters.

"Are you sure? What if I told you your favorite people were already there?" Ian smiled.

"I thought they had eyes on Strasser's lab?" I asked.

"They do. They're running the technical side from the safe house while the tactical team is on the ground near the lab," Ian explained.

"And Adam is okay with that?"

"If he wants to move into a team leader position, he'll have to be," he told me. "I told Thatcher that I wanted the Bologna team back together. We work well together, and it seemed like a good transition for you as you entered the field."

"Thank you, Ian."

"It's what I do."

I laughed. "What, exactly, is it that?"

"I assemble a competent, completely badass team of agents to catch bad guys," he smirked.

"You're not going to start wearing an eye patch, are you?"

"I might."

"I can live with that."

We were about to turn left and follow the walkway to the car when I saw them. Wren and Char were walking hand in hand, like an ordinary couple taking in the sites of this beautiful and historic city. They may have looked like a happy couple, but my suspicions had been confirmed. In my flat he had stressed to Wren the importance of going to her father in Brussels. There was no reason for him to bring her to Bruges unless he had convinced her to pursue whatever it was she was supposed to lead us to.

"Ian!" I grabbed his arm. "They're here."

Ian turned his body around as only a stealthy agent could. "Where?" I pointed to them across the square.

"What's the plan?" I asked.

"Follow me." Ian's directive was quick and concise. I did as he said and mirrored his steps along the far side of the square from Wren and Char until we were parallel to them. A woman exited the lace shop we loitered in front of and said something that sounded less than complimentary to us in French, which made me kick myself for not having taken Thatcher's suggestion that I study up on my Rosetta Stone more seriously. We shuffled a few more feet and then stopped.

"Now what?" I asked.

"Now we wait."

We stopped just outside a crowded café and stood in the shadow of the awning and watched them. A line was forming outside of the bell tower, but it moved at a steady pace. It didn't take long for Char and Wren to disappear inside the historical structure. Our gaze moved to the window on the second floor. As I suspected, it was difficult to make out exactly who was in the window. But Ian, being the well-prepared agent that he was, retrieved a device from his pocket to remedy our dilemma. He pulled at either end of the small, rectangular box, elongating it. Then he put it up to his eyes.

"What's that?" I asked jealously. "And why don't I have one?"

"Mini binoculars. And I'll make sure you're issued one when we get back. Stop whining." Ian handed me the binoculars, and I focused on the window in the tower. Within minutes, Wren appeared. Her arms lifted to the loose brick where she was used to finding notes from her father. But this time, the only thing she would find was rubble. Wren's body jerked to the side and Char came into view. He shoved his hand in the empty space in the wall and confirmed that Wren had found nothing. He focused his angry gaze to the window so Wren couldn't see his face.

"That is not the face of Prince Charming," I told Ian.

Like us, he was sure her father would have left a clue for her there. Whatever he had riding on this was slipping through his fingers, and his agitation was rising. Char composed himself, painted a smile on his face, and then turned around.

I handed the device back to Ian. "They're on their way back down."

Char and Wren shot from the exit door and started across the square, Wren's hand again in Char's firm grasp. Ian nodded his head to the left, indicating it was time to move. We stayed a safe distance as we followed along the side of the square. They curved to the left and appeared to be headed for an adjacent street. We were ten feet away from saving Wren from the trouble she didn't know she was in when a waiter tripped, sending a tray of dirty dishes crashing to the ground. The noise echoed off the buildings and caused hundreds of necks, including Wren and Char's, to snap in our direction. Char's eyes locked on mine and a sinister grin turned up the corners of his mouth. My gut twisted … again.

Wren looked at me sympathetically. "I'm sorry. I have to get to my father," was all she said before she and Char took off running.

They raced around the corner and onto a pedestrian street, and I was sure we had them. I was wrong. A tourist group—flag-waving leader and all—was herding toward us. Char and Wren disappeared into the sea of people. Like salmon swimming upstream, Ian and I fought our way through the crowd, emerging just in time to watch Char open the back door of a black car on the corner of an adjacent street.

"Wren!" I shouted, but it was too late. She looked at me briefly before she and Char scurried into the backseat. The door closed behind them just as it pulled away from the curb and sped away.

Thinking quickly, Ian spotted a delivery van and informed the driver in no uncertain terms that we would be commandeering his vehicle. Translation: Ian pulled the driver from the vehicle and shouted something to him in French. I jumped in the passenger seat and Ian peeled off down the street behind Wren.

"Buckle up," he instructed.

"Aren't you glad we already upgraded this mission from a boring babysitting job?" I readied my gun and rolled the window down.

"Think you can hit it this time?" Ian said as he maneuvered down the street.

"Really? You wanna be snarky right now?" I countered. "It was dark!" A satisfied smile appeared on Ian's face.

Ian raced toward the car that was carrying Wren. There were people on one side of the street and cars parked along the other, which made for limited navigating options.

CRASH.

Ian side swiped a car and knocked its mirror off.

CRACK.

And another.

SMASH.

There went my mirror.

"Is there a point system here I'm not aware of?"

Ian zoomed on without a word. Finally, we left the close quarters of the side streets of Bruges behind and increased our speed on the open road. "Think they know we're following them?" I asked. My question came just seconds before Char leaned out of the left side of the car and shot at us, the bullet dinging off our roof.

"Will that suffice as an answer?" Ian replied.

I let out an exasperated breath. "Tires, right?" I said, confirming my target as I did my best to steady my arm in the open window frame. Ian nodded and I fired my first shot. It missed.

Wren's car flew ahead. We followed them around a corner and onto what turned into a desolate road. The delivery van we had procured was having trouble keeping up, but with no other cars on this road, we managed to gain a few car lengths.

Misplaced confidence filled me until Char shot again. A spider web of cracks appeared when his bullet pierced the window.

"Are you hit?" Ian shouted.

"No, I'm okay. But that was way too close for comfort!" I fired back at their car and sent the driver's side mirror flying. Sparks flew off their back fender when I fired again.

Half of Char's body appeared out the window of their car this time. He raised his gun and smiled at me eerily. I aimed my weapon at him, and we fired simultaneously. Contrary to my training, I had been aiming for his head, but got a direct hit on his shoulder instead. His body jerked back, and I thought he might fall completely out of the window. No such luck. He slid back into the car just as our vehicle began to wobble.

We rocked back and forth as Ian tried to realign us. We began to spin. Suddenly, we tipped completely onto the passenger side. Our momentum propelled us along the pavement. Metal screeched on the asphalt, sending sparks flying, and shattered glass all around me. I awkwardly wedged my foot near the top of the van to keep my body from making contact with the rough pavement. Smoke billowed from the engine and started to fill the van. By the time we came to a dead stop, the gray curtain choked my lungs and clouded my sight.

"Ian!" I called through my coughs. No answer. I called his name again and reached out in search of him. My outstretched hands groped through the smoke, landing on his limp body. "Oh God. C'mon, stay with me, Ian!" I unbuckled his seatbelt, and his lifeless body fell into me. Maneuvering my body behind the passenger seat, I pulled Ian and dragged him to the back of the van. My efforts to move his strong, solid body were a reminder of how much further I had to go in my strength training. I kicked one of the back doors open. It crashed to the ground with a loud, metallic ding.

Fear and adrenaline raging through my body were the only things that enabled me to pull Ian from the van as quickly as I did. His head was clear of injury except for a cut near his hairline, which was obviously a result of the crash. Laying him flat, I checked his body for wounds. His shirt was bloodied, so I ripped it from him to find the point of entry of Char's bullet.

There was so much blood that I had to swipe Ian's shirt across his chest to find the bullet entry point. Small cuts from glass wept blood, but the penny-shaped hole high on the left side of his chest oozed with thick, red fluid. I balled up Ian's shirt and began applying pressure to the wound. I didn't know what else to do.

"Please don't die, Ian." I wiped tears and dirt from my face. "I should have told you this before. I love you, too," I whispered. "So much."

I took three deep breaths and composed myself. I needed to find Ian's phone and call Claudia, but I was afraid to release the pressure I was keeping on Ian's wound.

"Okay," I said aloud. "You can do this, Vic." I pressed one hand on the bloody cloth and began searching Ian's pockets with my free hand.

"Now really isn't the time to get frisky, Victoria." Ian's raspy voice was music to my ears.

"Oh my God! Ian!" I threw my body over his and kissed him hard. He winced. "Oh! I'm sorry! Are you okay?"

"Well, thanks to your quick thinking to put pressure on my wound, I'm better than I could have been."

"I was looking for your phone so I could call Claudia," I told him. The wind blew smoke from the van in our direction, burning my eyes. I rubbed them and waited for the breeze to pass.

"It's in my back pocket."

I retrieved Ian's phone and found Claudia's number. "Claudia, it's Vic." I told her what happened and where I thought we were. I heard the clacking of her keyboard, and within seconds she had pinpointed our location through Ian's phone.

"Adam is on his way," I said.

"Good," Ian said. "Because when we get back to the safe house, you're going to have to get this bullet out of my chest." Then he passed out.

Chapter 9

Ian leaned on Adam as we walked through the door to the safe house. He had passed out twice in the car, so the fact that he was walking somewhat on his own gave me hope. We rushed to the couch, and Adam helped Ian lie down. We had balled up Ian's shirt and used it to apply pressure to his wound. At first it worked well, but by the time we got to the safe house, the once-white shirt was soaked red with blood.

"You said I'd have to pull the bullet out of your chest," I said. "Why aren't we taking you to a hospital?"

"There's no time," Adam answered. "Hospitals have this pesky thing about wanting to follow procedure and monitor you. We dig it out, staple him up, and we're back on the road."

I knew I was staring at Adam like a deer in headlights, but I couldn't blink. He just told me I had to dig out the bullet that was lodged in Ian's chest like it was no big deal. I thought I had seen a lot of shit during my days living in a seedy part of Miami, but retrieving a bullet from someone's body would blow all of it away.

"Okay. But who's really going do it?" I asked as Claudia propped Ian's legs up on two cushions.

"You are." Ian's reply was matter of fact.

"You were serious about that?"

"We'll talk you through it, but you have to do it." I hadn't heard such a somber tone from Claudia before.

"Why?" I asked desperately.

"Because it may just be you and someone else out there another time, and you won't have a choice," Claudia said. "Trust me. I know."

I took the deepest breath in the history of deep breaths and said, "Okay. Show me what to do." Claudia set a tool kit in front of me. I knelt next to Ian, unzipped the case, and opened it like a book. My eyes scanned the tools and landed on the pliers. "I'm guessing these are going to be my best bet."

Adam nodded and I slid them out of the case. Claudia uncovered the wound on Ian's chest and poured half a bottle of water directly on it. As soon as the liquid hit, a groan escaped Ian's lips.

Claudia placed her hand on Ian's head. "It's okay, Ian. It's okay," she said calmly.

I held the pliers in my hand, my eyes darting between the tool and Ian.

"You can do this, Victoria." Ian squeezed my hand. His confidence in me was great, but I was only confident that I was about to root around in his chest and cause more damage than the bullet had.

Claudia poured more water on Ian's wound and followed it with another clear solution. It bubbled up and spilled across his chest. Ian winced again with a clenched jaw.

"Okay, Vic," Adam began. "Look in the wound and feel around the perimeter." I steeled myself and did as he said. When I pressed my fingers down along the inflamed area, a hard knot rolled beneath his skin.

"I can feel it!" My voice chirped with excitement like I had just won the lottery.

"Great. Now, with your fingers here, use the pliers and reach in for the bullet." Adam instructed me with the same calm demeanor as he had when training me to use firearms. He was an excellent and patient teacher.

My lungs filled to capacity as I looked down at the wound and then at Ian's face. He nodded ever so slightly. With my breath held, I inserted the pliers, found the bullet, and pulled it out slowly. Ian screamed in agony and then passed out.

My eyes felt as big as saucers. "Oh my God! Ian!"

"He's okay," Claudia said. "Passing out is the best thing for him right now."

I let out a heavy breath. "I did it." I'm not sure I had ever been so amazed with myself.

"You did it," Adam said with a proud smile.

"Well done, Vic," Claudia praised.

"It didn't seem like it was very deep," I said.

"It passed through the windshield before it hit him, which slowed it down a bit," Adam explained.

Adam stepped away and returned quickly with what looked like a can of Fix-A-Flat. He took the tube attached to the nozzle, placed it gently at the entrance of Ian's wound, and then pulled the trigger. A yellowish cream filled the place once occupied by a bullet. Adam wiped it with a clean cloth and then used a surgical staple gun to secure close the hole.

"What was is that?"

"It's a foam that heals wounds from the inside out. It works with the body's chemistry to prevent bleeding out and then repairs the injury," Adam answered. "It's pretty common in the military."

"It's amazing! Is he going to be okay?" I asked.

"He's going to be just fine. This isn't his first gunshot wound," Claudia said.

I nodded and rubbed my eyes before running my fingers through my ratted hair. Adam and Claudia returned to their duties while I sat on the floor next to Ian and waited for him to wake up. Unlike my time at the safe house in Padova, I was happy to have nothing to do. Back then my idle time was plagued with wondering where my brother was. Now I was waiting on the man I loved to wake from his pain-induced sleep so we could carry on with my first mission as a secret agent. My, how times had changed.

I racked my brain for the next move in finding Wren. After the shoot-out on the highway, I could only imagine that Wren was scared to death. Char had shown his true colors and gotten off his white horse. Having not found anything at the bell tower, what would Char do with her? Would he take her to the lab, or was there another hiding place they planned on getting the missing information out of her? The problem was, she didn't have a clue what was going on.

"I'm incredibly proud of how you handled yourself today," Ian whispered.

"You're awake!" I shot to my knees and spun around. "I'm just glad you're okay."

"I'll be just fine." Ian pushed himself upright and then stood slowly. "Got a clean shirt around here?" he asked Adam. Adam brought him a plain, black t-shirt. I helped him put it on since his shoulder was still sore.

"How are you supposed to do anything while you're healing? You can barely get yourself dressed," I said.

"Don't worry. That goo they filled the wound with will have me healed in less than twenty-four hours," he replied.

"That's why the military developed it," Adam added. "Can't have our men down for too long."

While Ian had been sleeping, Claudia gathered information on Strasser and the medical research company he worked for.

"Thatcher had me pull everything I could on both Strasser and the research facility," Claudia began. "It's a well-known place called the Regal Institute. By all accounts, this place is on the up and up. Strasser's been there for a couple of years doing what he does best: researching infectious diseases. Every report he's signed off on is totally legit."

"So they've covered their tracks then?" I asked.

"Oh ye of little faith!" Claudia smiled and raised an eyebrow. "They're your standard medical research company on the outside, but with a little digging and hacking into their sub-par security system—really, you'd think it'd be harder to crack—I found this." Claudia struck one last key on her laptop and spun it around for us to see.

"What are we looking at?" I asked.

"This is a string of emails between someone named Moreau and the head of infectious disease research, Conway Harrison."

I scanned through a few of the oldest emails. "There's little in here about actual medical research. It's all about Strasser. They hand picked him to develop a cure for a bacterial infection. That doesn't sound very nefarious."

"Keep going," Claudia said.

I scrolled and read further, my eyes widening as the realization of what they were planning came to light. "Oh my God. Is this saying what I think it is?"

"If you think it's saying that they're going to start a global outbreak and then extort billions from the governments of the world for the cure, then yes."

"That's why Strasser hid the cure. Without it, they can't release the infection. They'd all be doomed."

"Our number one priority is to find Wren," Ian said through a slightly strained voice. "Whoever gets to her first gets the cure. Adam, follow up with the rest of the Brussels team and see what they have from their watch of the Regal Institute. Claudia, I need the surveillance report for every square inch of roadway after the crash. Victoria, work with Claudia on that. Once you locate them, we need to know if Char has revealed his intentions to Wren yet. As long as he's still playing the White Knight, she's safe. If not, our clock will be ticking a lot faster." Ian moved faster than I thought one would after being shot. But as he said, it wasn't the first time he had been shot, and Ian was pretty badass, so it likely hardly fazed him at all.

We nodded at Ian's orders. Adam got on his cell and moved to another room. Claudia turned her laptop back toward her and began accessing every surveillance camera she could. I took a step toward Ian, but Claudia grabbed me by the wrist and shot me a look before I could get any further.

"Not now," she advised.

"I just want to check on him." I tried to hide the immediate defensiveness that rocketed through me.

"Not now." Claudia shot me a look that reminded me of my current objective to separate business from my personal life. Flipping the switch between those two lives was going to take some practice. I dipped my chin and turned my body and attention back to her.

"Have you found them?" I took a seat next to Claudia and rested my elbows on the table as we both peered at the screen.

"They circled around through some other rural roads and made their way back onto the E40 and headed straight to Brussels," she said. "It's only about an hour to Brussels from Bruges, so they're likely already there."

"Great, so we can find them on surveillance in Brussels, right?" I asked confidently.

"Not exactly. They got off the E40 just before Brussels." Claudia pointed at the square on the screen that showed Wren and Char's mysterious driver exiting the highway. "If they're in Brussels, they were smart and went in through back roads. I don't have eyes on them anywhere."

A defeated breath left me as I thought of what to do. Our objective was to ascertain if Wren knew she was in trouble or if Char was still putting on a show. I perused the screen in front of me. On it were four squares, each showing a different time lapse along the E40 of when Wren's car passed through. It zoomed through each frame so quickly that I couldn't see what was happening.

"Can I see the other surveillance angles?" I asked.

"Yeah. Gimme a sec."

Claudia pulled up the other surveillance sections from along E40 and changed the view to show six squares at a time. Then she rotated through the footage, showing six different scenes each time. She switched the views and found that at one point, they had hit a bit of traffic, which slowed them down to almost a complete stop.

"Give me just this frame," I said, pointing to the screen. The car inched into better view to where I could see through the side window. "Now freeze that. How do you zoom in?" Claudia circled the arrow around a plus sign in the right corner of the screen. I took the mouse in my hand and clicked until I saw what I was looking for.

"They're all cozied up in that back seat. Looks like she's okay," she said. She was right. It did look that way. Wren was leaning into Char and he had his arm around her.

It could be that she was fine, but I had to be sure. I fixed my eyes on every pixelated piece of that picture until I found what I hoped I would not.

"I wish that were the case. His gun." I pointed at the screen.

"He shot at you, Vic. His gun is still out."

"His gun isn't just out, it's pointed at her. You or I would rest the gun on our lap with our wrist touching our leg. Better yet, if we were out of danger, we'd holster our gun." I pulled my gun from my holster and demonstrated. "Like this. See, my gun is pointed in the direction of my knee. His wrist is resting against his stomach so the barrel is pointed at Wren."

"Damn it. She's in trouble." Claudia leaned back in her chair. Adam was still on his cell with the Brussels team, and Ian's voice began echoing from another room with statements that sounded like he was responding to Director Thatcher. "Hopefully Adam's got something from the team lead over at Regal."

I pressed my lips together and willed the wheels in my brain to turn. There had a to be a way to find Wren. Maybe it would start with finding the safe deposit our mystery key would fit into. *Pfft.* And maybe I'd find a needle in a haystack.

"So … while we're waiting…" I said casually to Claudia. "Any chance you found something on you know who?"

She took a deep breath and whispered a hesitant, "Maybe."

My heart began to race. Since the moment Ian told me my brother was dead, my motivation for becoming a Rogue agent was so that I could one day find Damon and make him pay. I never dreamed it might happen so quickly.

"Really?" I leaned forward with wide eyes.

"Don't get your hopes up," she cautioned. "He's moved around a lot in the last several months, and there's no pattern to where he goes. All I know is that right now, he's in Istanbul."

"Oh my God. I can't believe this. So what do we do now?" I asked impatiently.

"Slow down, woman. We're not *doing* anything. I'm *tracking* him, as in knowing his location. I don't have any other intel on what he's doing." Claudia began shoving papers into a manila folder. "Also, you may have noticed, we're in the middle of an assignment." She sighed. "I knew I shouldn't have agreed to do this. You're not ready. You're still too tender."

"I'm *not* too tender. I *am* ready," I protested.

She turned head to me and cocked it to one side as she looked at me with disbelief. "Vic, I'm sorry, but you're *not* ready. Everything boiling inside you is about vengeance. I get it, really, I do. I was there with you in the bakery that day. But you have to want to bring Damon down to bring justice to every life he's destroyed, not just yours."

Claudia waited patiently while I soaked up her words. My blood boiled with vengeance for how Damon destroyed everything that mattered to me. The only thing I wanted was to avenge my brother's death. Gil deserved that. But she was right. It couldn't be about just my tragedy.

"This is really hard, Claudia," I said, fighting back tears of pain and anger.

"I know," she said softly. "Let's just get through this assignment first, then ... I'll see what I can do. How's that?" she offered.

"That sounds great."

"What sounds great?" Ian asked as he stepped into the room. I whipped around in time to see his unsuspecting expression.

"Claudia had some wild fling in Monte Carlo and I'm trying to dig up the dirt. She promised to fill me in when we finish this assignment," I told him. It seemed like a viable excuse. He had just walked into a room with two whispering girlfriends who hadn't really seen each other in months.

"O-kay," Ian replied awkwardly. My excuse seemed to have done the trick in getting Ian to step away from asking any more questions. "Well then ... perhaps you can continue the slumber party conversation later."

"Absolutely," I said. "How are you feeling?"

"I'm fine, Victoria. And, I do have to say, you did a much better job retrieving the bullet your first time than Claudia did." He winked. Claudia smiled and shook her head as she shifted her laptop so Ian could get a better angle. "What do we have?"

"They took the E40 to Brussels but got off before they entered the city. They could be anywhere at this point," she told him.

"And what about the E40 surveillance?" Ian asked.

"We pulled this from a point when they got held up in traffic." I indicated to the laptop screen and to the gun Char held at Wren.

"Bye-bye, Prince Charming." Ian put his hands on his hips just as Adam entered the room. "Got anything?" he asked Adam.

"The team with eyes on the lab says there's been nothing out of the ordinary. No one has come or gone for two days."

"*That* is out of the ordinary," I said. "You've been watching a location for two days and no one has come or gone?"

"Places like this frequently have residence quarters. Their work is so intense and time constrictive that they sleep for small periods of time there at the facility," Adam explained.

"Really?"

"Really."

"Yeah, but there has to be nonmedical, administrative staff that doesn't stay overnight. You checked the schematics of the building? There's no underground tunnel like at the safe house outside Bologna?" I asked.

"There's nothing on the schematics and no official records of tunnels being constructed in the last twenty years." Claudia's answer came like an apology. "But we're waiting on the infrared satellite image to confirm."

"Let me know as soon as you have that," Ian said authoritatively. "Victoria and Claudia, get me a list of possible banks for this safe deposit key."

I worked with Claudia for the next few hours on compiling a list of banks in Belgium with safe deposit boxes, as well as those across Europe that make them available to foreign residents. It was a massive list, but we nailed it down to a radius of locations that Strasser could have feasibly accessed to leave information for Wren. Claudia hacked into each bank's system one at a time and searched for both Jeremy *and* Wren Strasser. It took hours because we had to match up the scanned signature card with Jeremy Strasser's signature. The painstakingly long process finally paid off when we found the right Jeremy Strasser's safe deposit box in a bank in Ghent.

"Thank you, sweet baby Jesus!" Claudia said as she lined up the signature on Strasser's military id with the one on file for with the bank in Ghent. "It only took a hundred and forty-seven tries, but we found it." She leaned back in chair with a satisfied grin on her face.

"Hey, Ian! Time to flash that badge of yours again," I called to him. "Claudia found the safe deposit box."

"Good work, Claudia," he said as he entered the room. "Where is it?"

"Europabank in Ghent," she answered with a smile.

"Oh, thank God," Ian sighed.

"What?" I asked, puzzled why Ian seemed so relieved.

"We're in Gentbrugge, which is all of fifteen minutes from Ghent. It's nice to have something be easy for a change," he sighed.

"Don't get your hopes up, boss. This branch has not only signature verification, but photo id as well," Claudia warned.

"Dammit!" Ian sat at the table across from Claudia and threaded his fingers together.

"What's the problem? We'll walk in, you'll flash your badge, show them the key, and they'll let us in." I didn't understand why Ian was upset. He was acting like we had hit a brick wall in the mission.

"I can clear a room of unsuspecting tourists, Victoria. I can't walk in and demand entry into a secured area of an international bank without a warrant," he explained.

I came behind Claudia just to see what she was looking at, not that I could fix or change anything. The photo of Wren's father was last updated six months ago. Remembering how he looked in the video, it seemed he hadn't changed much, except for a few more gray hairs. But the photo of Wren was dated five years ago when she was sixteen. You could tell it was her, but she definitely looked different now.

"Then I'll be Wren," I said matter-of-factly.

"What?" Ian furrowed his brow at me.

Claudia looked at the picture of the teenage Wren on her screen and then looked at me. "Holy crap. She could. A quick dye job and she could pass for her now."

"No," Ian declared.

"We need to know what's in that safe deposit box," I countered.

"You're not trained to go undercover, Victoria. I'm not going to throw you in there like that." Ian stood up and walked to the other side of the room.

"This isn't the mob, Ian. It's a bank. Wren clearly hasn't been there in years. No one will know the difference." I stared at Ian, waiting for him to reply, but he just stared back at me. I closed the distance between us, not caring that Claudia was right there or that Adam just emerged from the bedroom where he had been working. I spoke quietly. "You said you weren't going to treat me differently than any other agent. If Wren slightly resembled Claudia, you'd throw her in as Wren's double in a heartbeat. My job is to be a contributing member of this team. Let me do my job."

"She's English. What about the accent?" he argued. He knew I was right and that sending me in was our best hope of helping Wren and her father, but he had to grasp for one last straw.

"I've been with you for the last four months, and three of those months were spent immersed in British culture. I'm pretty sure I've picked up on a few things." I paused. "What do you think, Claudia?" I said in what I thought was a spot on British accent.

"It's good, but Ian can help you hone it," Claudia said.

"And if she slips at all, she can cover by saying that she just spent a year in the States and picked up some bad habits," Adam added.

"I can throw in a *bollocks, wanker,* and *cheerio* if you'd like." I steadied my gaze at Ian, hoping he'd see that I was ready and able to do whatever I needed to do.

"Fine," he finally said. "But keep your conversation to a minimum. Be quick. Just pull everything from the box and we'll sort though it back here." Ian was curt, but I brushed it off.

Ian looked so conflicted. I wanted to remind him that he had trained me well. I was nervous and scared and all the things an agent should be the first time they did something like this. I wanted to remind him I was the girl who was determined enough to shoot herself so the team could take down Damon and his men. If I could survive that, impersonating a British college student was going to be a piece of cake.

Chapter 10

The next morning when Claudia and I emerged from the bathroom after dying my hair, Adam and Ian were sitting at the table with Carter. *Oh, Carter.* We'd had such a love-hate relationship in Italy. I hadn't seen him since they all escorted me from my hospital room.

"Hot damn! You look good as a red head, Vic!" Carter bellowed as he stood to greet me. He wrapped his arms around me and Ian shot him a look.

"Can you *not* be yourself right now, Carter?" I said to him.

"I missed you, too, girl!" He squeezed me even tighter. "And, seriously, you pull the red off really well. You should consider keeping it after this assignment."

"Duly noted," I said, laughing. "What are you doing here?"

"I'm leading the team covering the Regal Institute with some ex-military guys," he began.

"Aren't you guys all ex-military?"

"Yeah, but these guys aren't Rogue or even INTERPOL. Thatcher brings these guys in when we need extra manpower and brute force. I'm totally kickass and all, but these guys? Even *I'm* intimidated by them."

"Wow. Although, you could take down the enemy by overwhelming him with your charming personality," I quipped.

"True." Carter gave me that sarcastic crooked smile of his and continued. "Adam thought it best for me to come in and brief you guys on where we are on the assignment." Carter sat back down, and that was when I noticed the blueprints for the lab spread over the table. "We got the full schematics and radar satellite imaging for the building and the surrounding area. There are two tunnels, about a half a mile each, extending here and here, but you have to enter here to access both." Carter pointed to two almost translucent tubes jutting out from the darker building.

"What are these?" I asked of the small squares that accented one of the tunnels like climbing spikes on an old telephone pole. "They aren't on the other tunnel. Are these rooms?"

"That's what they appear to be. They may be sleeping quarters," Ian explained.

I took a longer look at the building plan as a whole. It was massive with two wings on either side. There was a loading dock in the back and two specific parking areas: one centrally located in front of the building as would be expected at any place of business and a smaller lot closer to the south wing.

"No. The sleeping quarters are here." I circled the south wing of the building with my finger. "Look at the plumbing lines that go out from the whole building except for in the tunnels. If those rooms are for sleeping, this is the worst design ever. No bathrooms for a quarter mile? There's a second parking lot in this part of the property. It could be executive offices, but I'm more inclined to think it's the residence quarters."

"So if this is the residence wing of the facility, then what are these rooms? Storage?" Adam proposed.

"Could be. Could be worse. If they're holding Strasser against his will, maybe he's there," I suggested. "And it's likely that's where they'll take Wren."

"They have Strasser's daughter?" This was news to Carter.

"We think so. Wren's conveniently recent boyfriend showed up when we were getting ready to leave for London. Long story short, he came with us and then they disappeared yesterday morning. We caught up with them in Bruges, had a car chase and a shoot out, and crashed the van Ian commandeered. He also shot Ian, and I got to dig out the bullet. So, it was super secret agenty!" I said with a sugary smile.

Ian ignored my sarcasm and moved the conversation along. "Suffice it to say, Victoria's gut instinct that we couldn't trust him was right from the start."

"If there's anything I know about Vic, it's that her gut is spot on. If she says the boyfriend is not a friendly, just tell me when you want me to aim and shoot." Carter nodded at me.

"My gut thanks you." I chuckled.

"I can tell you, though, they haven't brought her to the lab. We've had eyes on every door as well as the tunnel entrance over the last twenty-four hours."

"There's probably a rendezvous point, and they just haven't connected yet. Keep your eyes on the lab," I said. "We'll head to the bank and find out what Strasser is hiding, hopefully before they make another move."

"Carter, keep me posted," Ian instructed. "I want to know the moment you see anything. Claudia, I want facial recognition run on all the cameras inside as well as the area surrounding the bank. I don't know who else might know about the safe deposit box, and I'm not taking any chances. You let me know if anyone pops up. Adam, you're coming with us. An extra pair of eyes and an extra trigger finger is always helpful." Ian moved around the apartment collecting items needed for our mini road trip to Ghent: Wren's file, the new ID he made from the picture Claudia took as soon as I was officially a red head, a messenger bag for me to put any and all pertinent information in from the box and, of course, the key to the safe deposit box.

The three of us piled into the car, me sitting in the back of the two-door sports car since I was the smallest. I turned on the English accent I had been practicing as soon as Ian pulled onto the street and recited some phrases.

"'Ello. My nayme is Wren Strassah."

"Too cockney. Again," Ian directed. I hated how curt he could be with his directions, but I followed orders and tried it again and again until I sounded more like Princess Kate than a character from *Oliver*.

"Hello. My name is Wren Strasser. I'd like to access my safe deposit box, please."

"Good. That's good. Keep that phrasing and cadence in your head and you'll be fine. You're not there to make friends and be chatty. Keep conversations short, and we'll be in and out of there in no time," Ian said, finally giving his approval.

Adam pulled up to the curb as Ian was calling Claudia. "How's the facial recognition coming? Got anything?" He *mmhmm'd* a few times, told her to let him know if anything *did* come up, and then ended the call.

"Nothing?" Adam asked as he handed something back to Ian.

"No," Ian confirmed. Ian placed the small com device in his ear.

"Don't I get one of those?" I asked.

"Claudia will communicate with me if anyone shows up on the facial recognition," he answered. "You just focus on your accent and getting in and out of the vault as quickly as possible."

He opened his door, pulled his seat forward, and helped me climb out. I straightened the plaid tunic I wore over black skinny jeans and twisted the shaft of my boots to a more comfortable place. Adam handed me my gun, and I slipped it into the holster of my compression shorts. I remember laughing at Claudia when she first showed them to me. I thought she was punking me, but these things were no joke. I would swap wearing cute panties any day of the week for these things.

With the satchel crossing my body, I nodded at Ian and took two steps toward the bank.

"Wait." Ian grabbed my elbow and tugged me so I turned around. "How are you?"

"I'm fine." I furrowed my brow at him.

"Good." He looked like he may have had something else to say, but decided against it.

"Trust me, Ian."

"I do trust you." Ian caught my eyes as if he just realized the moment was real. We had trained for months, and now I was actually in the field. He placed a soft kiss on my lips and then smiled confidently. "Then let's get this over with so we can find Wren. They primarily speak Dutch here, but they may speak French, so I'll do the talking at first and find someone who speaks English."

We walked into the bank and were immediately greeted by a tall man wearing a sharp suit. His thin, gray hair told me he was probably in his sixties. He held one arm bent with a pen in his hand and swung his other arm as he strode from the sleek glass podium to meet us.

"Hoe kan ik u helpen?" the man asked.

"Spreek je Engles?" Ian said to him.

"Yes, of course. Good afternoon. Welcome to Europabank. I am Albert Booten, the bank manager. How may we be of assistance today?" he asked politely.

I took a little breath before I spoke. "I'd like to access my safe deposit box, please." Ian smiled at me and gave my back a little rub to reassure me that I had done well.

"Yes, of course. We'd be happy to assist you with that today. We'll just need to see some identification," the gentleman advised. We followed him to the end of the long desk of bank tellers next to the entrance to the vault at which time I handed him the driver's license Ian had manufactured for me a little over an hour ago. "Miss Strasser! Oh my! How could I not have recognized you? You've grown up quite a bit since I last saw you."

I smiled nervously. I had hoped the turnover rate at this bank was high enough to have seen several bank managers come and go in the last several years. No such luck.

"Oh, it's quite all right. I'm sorry I don't remember you." Easier to play that card up front than try to follow along with any walks down memory lane Mr. Booten may want to take.

"Oh, I wouldn't expect you to remember an old man like me!" He laughed. "Now don't let me hold you up. Let me just get your signature card." He took my ID and walked into a back room. It took him about five minutes to locate Wren's signature card and the second key to the box. When he returned, his mood had gone from jovial to all business. Something was off.

"Everything all right?" I ask him.

"Uh … yes. Everything is in order here. Sorry it took me longer than I anticipated. If you'll sign this and then follow me," he instructed. I put the pen to the signature card and stared for a moment. It was going to be easier to forge Wren's signature than I thought. At sixteen her penmanship wasn't as fully developed as the recent handwriting samples I studies and traced in the car. I signed the card with the panache of a grown woman, and Ian and I followed Mr. Booten toward the vault without hesitation.

"I'm sorry, sir," Booten said. "Only the owner of the safe deposit box is permitted inside the vault."

Ian was about to protest the limitation when I put my hand on his chest. "It's all right, darling. I won't be but a moment." I smiled to remind him that we had already agreed I would sort through whatever was in the box and put everything I could in the messenger bag I had slung across my body.

"Right. I'll just wait here, then," Ian said reluctantly. I kissed him on the cheek and left him standing in the lobby of the bank.

Passing through a hallway on the way to the vault, I noted two doors on either side. One had to be a supply closet, as it was on the same side as the lobby and there wouldn't be enough room for an office. The other door, I assumed, was an office, break room, or copy room. We finally reached the vault itself. I thought it funny how it looked just like an actual vault that you'd see in the movies. The massive round door was swung wide open, but I could still see the polished ten-spoke handle that one would turn like a captain's wheel to open the enormous door.

The room containing the safe deposit boxes wasn't as large as I thought it would be. There appeared to be a hundred brass boxes lining the walls. I wondered what each box contained. Did others treat them like treasure boxes to hold not only their valued possessions, but also the secrets that could save someone's life?

I took in Mr. Booten again and saw that he looked upset. His eyes darted around and sweat glistened where his hairline used to be.

"Are you sure you're all right?" I asked.

"Yes, of course. Here we are!" Mr. Booten declared as he pointed to the box with the number forty-five engraved in it. It sat midway up the wall at a convenient location for retrieving it. He handed me my key and motioned for me to put it in the keyhole while he did the same with its counterpart. We turned them at the same time and released the lock.

"Thank you so much for your help. I'm sure I won't be long," I said to him as a polite way of scooting him along.

"Take your time, Miss Strasser," he said as he walked toward the door. Just as he was about to cross the threshold of the vault, he turned and whispered, "Don't worry. You're going to be just fine."

I smiled as if I knew what he was talking about, but my gut was rumbling. I didn't know why, so I got to work and slid the long box out from the wall and set it on the table. It was heavy, but not unbearably so.

Lifting the lid revealed a small envelope with Wren's name on it on top of a stack of various papers. Just as I reached into the box, Booten returned. *What happened to "take your time?"*

"Miss Strasser?" he said softly. I shoved the letter in my back pocket and pushed the other papers back into the safe deposit box. "Miss Strasser?"

"Yes," I replied. "Is everything all right?" I asked for the third time.

"Everything is fine." He smiled and I pushed the long box back into its slot. I had to hope that the letter on top was what Strasser needed Wren to find. We turned our keys and locked it back into place before stepping out of the vault. "I have something for you to sign before you leave."

"I signed the card before we came in," I reminded him.

"This is a different card. A, uh, new exit procedure," he stumbled. Something was definitely off. Wrong was more precise. Did he know I wasn't Wren? Had I been caught? If so, I was confident Ian would take care of it, but I slowed my gait to better take in my surroundings just in case. The door to the room I had earlier assumed was a break room or office was open. Mr. Booten stood to the side of that doorway and motioned for me to go in.

"Let me just tell my friend that I'll be another minute. I'd hate for him to worry," I said as I worked to step away from him.

"There's no time," he said quickly as he pulled me into the room. He held my arm tightly in his grasp, making it impossible for me to reach my gun. He shut the door behind us, and I was trapped. "It's going to be all right, Miss Strasser." He looked at me with compassionate eyes, and I became even more confused.

"That's the second time you said that to me. If it's in reference to something from when I was younger, I'm terribly sorry that I don't remember." I tried to move toward the door, satisfied that I had explained my lack of connection to his statement, but he stood in front and wouldn't let me leave.

"Oh, no, no, no! I'm sorry if I frightened you. They said you might be a bit distraught. I was just trying to calm you," he explained.

"Who said I might be distraught?" I put my hand on my waist, pulling the side of my tunic up to have easy access to my gun without actually pulling it out. Booten was acting like he was doing me some kind of favor, but it didn't make sense.

He didn't get a chance to answer because the explanation revealed itself from behind a hidden panel in the wall. A stocky man built like a bodyguard entered the room and immediately laid kind eyes on me. I could see the bulkiness of his holster under his arm and knew that it was too late to pull my gun.

"Wren," the man said softly. He was an American. He showed me his hands as he spoke; another telltale sign that he was definitely carrying. There's no reason to show someone your empty hands if there's no chance of you filling them with your preferred Glock. "I need you to listen to me. Your father sent me to get you. You're in grave danger."

Chapter 11

Of course I was in grave danger. Whoever this man was, he thought *I* was Wren, which told me that he didn't know her at all. It also told me that Strasser's boss had made sure no stone would be unturned and hired multiple bounty hunters to find Wren. I was a good pass for her with someone who had only been given her description or hadn't seen her in over five years, but not to someone who knew Wren or had studied any kind of recent picture of her. This guy was definitely the former.

I thought through my options. The room was too small to try and make a run for it, and there was no way to get Ian's attention. The size of the room also limited my ability to draw my gun. Once I did that, my mystery savior would draw his as well, and any gunfire would likely leave Mr. Booten, and possibly me, dead. However, my secondary thoughts laid out a plan that may get me into the lab to find Strasser. Carter's team was watching, so they would know I was there. Well, they'd know there was movement, and when Ian told them I had disappeared, they would put two and two together. With no other options, I went along with it.

"What do you mean I'm in grave danger?" I played up the fear in my voice for added effect.

"The people you're with are not who you think they are. Your father sent me and my team to get you, but when we got to Oxford you were already gone. When we lost track of you, your father suggested you might come here."

Wow. This guy was good. So they knew Wren had been picked up by Ian's team, but it was clear this guy had no idea who we were, and absolutely no clue that I was really a member of that team. They also were clueless to the fact that Char had Wren. That meant Char hadn't checked in with Strasser's boss yet. The question was, how did they know about the safe deposit box?

There was a commotion outside the room, distracting us all. I heard a loud voice say something in Dutch and then in English. Mr. Booten opened the door just enough to survey the situation. Behind him, Ian was having a verbal altercation with a bank employee at the end of the teller counter.

"No," he said condescendingly. "It is imperative that I retrieve my friend!"

"Sir, when she is done she will come back out. You are not permitted back there," the woman said with a polite, yet commanding tone.

At that moment, Ian turned and caught my eye through the two-inch gap in the door. I shook my head infinitesimally and darted my eyes to the right to tell him that we were not alone. I had a feeling he already knew something was wrong. Maybe my pretend savior popped up on the facial recognition scan Claudia had been running. It took only seconds for Ian to throw everything into the fire and bum rush the door. "Wren!" he called out to me as the mystery man slammed the door and yanked my arm toward him.

"There isn't time. We have to go now!" he shouted. I stumbled into him as we moved though the secret passageway he had entered through and down a circular stairway that was as old as the city of Ghent itself. I didn't say anything as I was trying to appear stunned at the whole situation, which wasn't entirely an act.

I heard Mr. Booten yelling at Ian that it was too late and that I—well, Wren—was now safe. That little tidbit of information would put Booten under an interrogation lamp for however long it took Ian to get the truth from him. At least Ian wasn't flying completely blind. He had to know that whoever had me was working for Strasser's boss and that I'd be on my way to the facility to be used as leverage against Strasser. Knowing that Carter's team had their eyes on the facility was helpful as well. When we arrived, they'd come looking for me.

With his fingers firmly wrapped around my wrist, I ran behind the man whose name I still did not know down a long, narrow corridor made of stone, and then up another flight of circular stairs and into an abandoned building through yet another secret passageway.

He dragged me behind him out onto the street until we reached a car. I twisted in his grip to get a look around me. We were at least two blocks from the bank. He opened the back door and shoved me inside before scooting in next to me. "Drive!" he said to the man behind the wheel.

"Are you going to tell me your name?" I asked, catching my breath.

"You can call me Mick," he said apologetically.

"And our driver? Does he have a name?"

"He prefers his anonymity."

"Right. So ... why did my father send you to come get me?" I asked. "I mean, was anything the other people told me true?" I had to play the now grateful girl who had been duped by the handsome Englishman.

"All I can tell you is that I was hired by your father to find you and take you to him. When you weren't in Oxford, I was told you would likely come to the bank. Really, it's best if you don't ask a lot of questions right now. We'll get you safely to your father's location and—"

"And what? I thought he was in danger. Why are you taking me *to* him?" I protested. I needed to know what he knew. I couldn't tell if he actually had information, or if he was just the delivery boy.

"I've already said too much. But don't worry. You're safe." Mick's answer was curt and woefully uninformative. He was either a great actor or truly thought he was bringing Wren to safety. Mr. Anonymity in the driver's seat turned his head slightly at my whining. Mick pulled a pack of gum from inside his jacket. He took out a piece, unwrapped it, and shoved the candy in his mouth.

"Mind if I have one?" I asked. Mick slid out another piece and handed it to me without saying a word. I shoved the gum in my mouth and the wrapper in my pocket. Then I put my head down and waited to arrive at our destination.

The seat pressed my gun against my spine. It made me feel secure, but I wasn't confident I'd get a chance to actually use it. I had to see how far I could get and what answers I could gather. I hoped that once we entered the secret tunnel that led to the lab compound—or brazenly walked through the front door, whichever Mick was instructed to do—no one else would be allowed in and the real Wren Strasser would be safe for a little while longer. But I didn't know how long I had before Char checked in to tell them he had Wren. Once that happened, the crap would surely hit the fan and I would face my consequences.

Until then, *I* was Wren, and I was going to get as close to saving Jeremy Strasser as possible.

"Where are we?" I asked after we had veered off the paved road and driven for another fifteen minutes. Neither of my companions answered. We approached a guard booth, and I was certain this was the entrance to the tunnel but … there was nothing there. Just dry, dusty ground. There was a chain link fence circling the nothing, beginning and ending at the guardhouse. Once the driver was identified, the gate of the fence slid to the side, making way for us. As it moved, so did the ground in front of us. The dirt bounced and shimmied around as the earth opened up like the Cave of Wonders and we drove in.

The cave was dark as we entered, but as the car moved further into the mouth of the tunnel, lights flickered on overhead. We drove until that leg of the tunnel ended and the second tunnel began to our left. Mick got out of the car and motioned for me to follow him. I slid out gingerly as I didn't want my gun to knock on the side of the car.

We stood there for a moment before two more men approached.

"Okay. I got her here. Where's the rest of my payment?" Mick asked.

Apparently our new friends felt it was starting to get crowded, so our driver remedied that. He reached inside his coat, retrieved a gun, and shot Mick in the head. I screamed, which was also not altogether an act. I had caused my own bloody scene in Italy, and part of my training with Ian included photos of a myriad of dead bodies in order to desensitize me to the shock of it all. But that moment brought out the truth of my telling Ian I would never get used to the horrors of this life.

Mick dropped to the ground like a limp noodle. I slammed backward into the car, letting tears roll down my face for effect. "Oh my God!" I cried.

"Let's go, sweetheart," one of the new thugs said as he grabbed my arm. He pulled me and we began to walk, leaving my silent driver and the other thug standing over Mick's dead body.

"Where are you taking me? I want to see my father!" I demanded. I tripped and began to fall, but was yanked back upright by the ridiculous strength of my captor.

"Oh, you're going to see him, all right," he barked at me. "There's a bounty on your head. First one to bring you in wins big, and we plan on cashing out." I wondered how long ago the bounty on Wren had been placed. My best bet was that it was around the same time Char showed up. The fact that he hadn't brought Wren in right away told me that maybe he had begun to really care for her. I guessed when Ian and I showed up, we reminded him of his potential cash-out and he stepped up his game. Then I thought about poor Mick. He had been so kind. And he seemed to think he was really saving me.

I tried to keep up the pace, afraid that if I fell behind again, my gun would somehow be discovered and then I'd be in a new world of trouble. As we moved around the corner to the other tunnel, there was an office with a large window in it looking out onto both corridors. Two guards were sitting in the booth, one of them with their eyes on a wall with six television monitors, the other one watching us. He winked at me and made me wish I had access to my gun so I could shoot the creepy smirk right off his face.

We walked about fifty yards down the tunnel and passed a few doors on either side before we reached another door on my right.

When we stopped, I questioned him again. "What are you going to do with me? Where is my father? Please! I don't understand what's going on!" I pleaded and whined.

"Shut up and wait here. You'll see your father soon enough." The metal door clanged and echoed as he slammed it, leaving me standing there alone and trembling. When I was sure he was gone, I checked for surveillance cameras. With no signs of any, I pulled myself together and then the gun from my back holster and checked it before returning it to its place. I would have to be ready with it sooner than later.

I went through the timeline of events from the moment I last locked eyes with Ian to the moment I watched my prison door slam. I estimated it was about an hour and a half. In that time Ian would have had Claudia expand the radius on the facial recognition from the street cameras as well as try to pinpoint where I may have exited with my captor. They would have found the car I was being held in and followed it as far as the street cameras would take them, running the plates in the mean time. If they weren't able to get a facial read on Mick or the driver, I could safely believe that the team would at least assume I'd be brought to the lab.

Mr. Booten would have also endured worse than the Spanish Inquisition from Ian. He would have been enlightened to reality of the situation and then provided all the information Ian required. For his sake, I hoped he'd get on board sooner rather than later. Ian wouldn't let the man's age deter him from getting information by whatever means necessary.

Ian would have also connected with Carter in that time. And, because Carter's team had eyes on the both the lab facility and the tunnel location, they would have seen the car come in. The problem would be that Carter wouldn't have had a clue it was me inside and not Wren until Ian told him so.

I didn't know how long I had before either the cavalry arrived or someone came to take me to Strasser. I gingerly tried the knob of the door and confirmed that it was locked. My eyes scoured the room. Dark, dingy cinder block walls surrounded me. The ceiling was just as disgusting, and there wasn't an air vent to be seen. At least there was a cot where I could sit, if I dared. God only knew what infestation was waiting for the lucky person who laid their head on its less than welcoming excuse for a pillow.

I breathed in the musty air and stretched my arms across my chest and my neck from side to side to loosen and warm up my muscles. Adam and Ian always got on me about not preparing my body before physical exercise. However this played out, I was about to be the most physically active I had ever been. It was not going to be a drill or a training exercise. My opponent's object was going to be to completely subdue and possibly kill me. And we were certainly not going out for drinks after we scuffled, as I had with Ian.

Fifteen, maybe twenty minutes passed without so much as the shuffling of feet outside the door. I wondered if they had gone to get Wren's father or if they were just trying to drive me crazy by isolating me before they took me to him.

The door flew open and I scurried back into a corner. I didn't know how many would be joining me, and I much preferred to survey the situation without someone being able to come up behind me. The same guy who escorted me to the room walked in alone, and then another man followed with a Glock firmly gripped in his left hand and Jeremy Strasser struggling to break free in his right.

Chapter 12

There was no doubt that the man they were holding was Jeremy Strasser. His goatee, bald head, and tattoos were just as they looked in the video he sent to Thatcher. The same fear that filled his eyes was present as well.

"Dad!" I shouted. I ran to him and threw my arms around him before the men could register the confused expression on Strasser's face. He knew I wasn't Wren but I couldn't give him even a second of time to question it. I buried my face into his neck and whispered, "Thatcher sent me."

He pulled me from him and took me in like a father would. "Oh my God, Wren! Are you okay?"

"I'm okay. Are *you* okay? I've been so worried!" I said. I turned toward the door and glared at our captors. "Let us out of here!" I charged at them, almost making it past them and through the door, but I was quickly shoved back and staring at the barrel end of their guns.

"I suggest you mind your manners," one of the muscled men said.

Before he could say anything else, a siren like a smoke detector on steroids sounded. The second man shot out of the room and returned within seconds.

Carter.

"There's a security breach in the main building." He started his report with a shout, but quickly altered his volume when the siren cut off.

"Looks like you two are going to be cozy in here a little while longer," the first thug said smugly. He bolted out of the room, letting the door swing shut behind him.

"Who are—" Strasser began.

"Shh!" I cut him off with a finger in the air. I studied the door and the knob closely, listening. It looked as if it had closed, but it was off just a hair, and I didn't hear it click. I drew my gun, then I carefully pulled the door until just a thin line appeared, giving me a small peek into the corridor. Inching it open further, and seeing that the coast was clear, I pulled my gum wrapper out of the hole in the strike plate.

"Who are you?" Strasser asked.

"My name is Vic Asher. I'm with the Rogue division of INTERPOL. Thatcher got your message and assembled one team to get Wren and another to help you," I whispered.

"Aren't you a little young to be a Rogue agent?" he observed.

"Yes. Yes, I am."

"So you're here for me, that means another team has Wren, right?"

"Something like that," I said vaguely as I peered through the crack in the door again.

"What does that mean?" His harsh voice cracked with despair. I didn't answer. Nothing I could have said in that moment would have made him feel any better about the situation, and my focus needed to be on getting us out of there and to a place where I could reasonably defend us.

"Is Wren safe?"

I still didn't answer. What was I going to tell him? His daughter was with a bounty hunter posing as her boyfriend?

"*Where* is my daughter?" he demanded.

I appreciated his need to know the status of his daughter, but we didn't have time for all the details. So I stepped closer to him and looked straight into his desperate eyes. "We only have a few minutes before those guys get back here. Now, you can either get me to a stairwell that will lead to the main building and the rest of my team, or we can hang out and chit-chat. I vote for option one. What about you?" I cocked my head to the side, raised my eyebrows, and waited for him to get on board.

"I ... I'm sorry. It's just ... she's all I've got."

I turned soft eyes to him. "It's okay. I'm sorry. Listen, we're doing everything we can to get you and your daughter to safety. In order to do that, you have to let me do my job. Now, are you familiar with this area of the compound?"

He thought for a moment before he answered. "Yes and no. I've never been this far into the tunnels before, but I know how to get back. Where exactly are we going?"

That was a good question. Carter's team would be looking for Strasser and me, but since the breach clearly didn't happen at the entrance to the tunnels, they'd be working their way from the main building down. The blueprints of the building showed a center atrium that served as a hub to all four wings of the facility. Carter's team would enter there so they could divide and conquer.

"We need to get to the main atrium of the building. Do you think you can lead us there?" I said.

"Yes, I think so," he answered a bit too hesitantly. "But ... you may see things along the way that, well, that are terrifying. They've been ... experimenting."

"Like, on people?" I shuddered at the thought.

"Yes. I ... I didn't know." I watched as that badass-looking genius held back tears. His fear was deep.

"All right then," I began. "Give me some basic directions here."

"The first stairwell door is just past the security booth on the left. That will take us to the first floor west hall, just off the main entrance."

"Great. Stay close."

I opened the door slowly. The halls were still empty. Thinking we were securely locked in, they must have all rushed to the security breach. And if Carter did what Carter does best, there would be a hell of a lot fewer guards returning to their posts down there.

Strasser did as he was told and stayed close. We scooted along the wall toward the security booth where the other tunnel was, my heart racing at an inhuman rate. I took inconspicuous deep breaths to calm myself as we moved. I had to be the strong Rogue agent I had presented myself as being.

We approached the security booth with caution. I held my gun up in a ready position, as prepared as I was ever going to be to defend Strasser and myself. The booth was empty, but that didn't seem right. The tunnels were empty, but they wouldn't have left the booth with no one to monitor the security camera feed.

We rounded the corner and were just steps away from the stairwell door when it flung open and a guard walked through. The guard and I looked at each other, both stunned. He looked as scared as I felt, and I could tell that he was a newbie to this world, the same as me. His hand was shaking and beads of sweat dotted his upper lip.

He pulled his gun, which made me nervous not because I was afraid of being shot, but because that shaky hand of his hadn't settled down. He didn't want to shoot me any more than I wanted to shoot him. It was like that scene in *The Sound of Music* when the family was escaping and it took Rolfe minutes to decide to whom he owed his devotion. I hoped I would fare better than the von Trapps.

"Where do you think you're going?" he asked. His voice trembled as he tried to be commanding.

"I'm getting this man to safety," I told him. "And you're going to let us pass."

"Oh really? Why … why would I do that?" He still wasn't sure of himself as I stared into his eyes, reiterating the gravity of my demand.

"Because you don't believe in what they're doing here. You thought you were taking a great security job with a high profile research lab. You had no idea who you were really working for and what they were capable of. My guess is that in the last two weeks, you've seen things you wish you could scrub from your memory, and what you really want is for someone to deliver you from this evil." I paused for a moment to allow my words to settle in. "What's your name?"

"Stevens."

"Well, Stevens, as you're aware, there is some seriously messed up shit going on in this lab. When everything hits the fan, and the media gets ahold of this, your name can either be in there as a hero or as one of the casualties. I *do not* want to have to shoot you, but I will do whatever I have to do to get this man to safety and save those who are being terrorized." I held my gun confidently in my hands while I watched Stevens do everything Adam ever told me *not* to do with the gun in his. "And I'm going to go out on a limb here and say that I've been given a lot more gun training that you have."

"They're literally going to kill me if they find out I just let you go," he stuttered as he lowered his weapon. I breathed a sigh of relief. An ill-prepared gunman is far more dangerous than a well-prepared one.

I lowered my weapon as well and stepped closer to Stevens. I carefully took the hand that still held his gun and pointed it at the vast, open space of the tunnel behind me. "Fire off two shots," I instructed.

"What?" he asked, confused.

"You'll need to have some kind of evidence that you at least tried to stop me," I told him.

"Oh, right, of course." He shot twice out into the tunnel and then lowered his gun again.

"Great. Now, don't be mad at me." With that, I shot Stevens in the leg. He cried out in pain and dropped to the floor. The bullet did little more than graze him, but it would be enough to hopefully prove that he didn't just let us get away.

"You did the right thing, Stevens!" I called as Strasser and I slid into the stairwell. I was sorry to leave Stevens lying there on the ground moaning in pain, but not sorry enough to go back and help him.

"You shot him!" Strasser said in shock. I was pleased to see that he was able to keep up with me as I climbed the stairs Ian Hale-style: two at a time.

"I grazed his leg," I said in my defense. "And I did it to help him. If things don't go our way up there, his boss is not going to be happy with him. That gun shot to the leg could save his life." Strasser didn't say anything else about it again. "Once we reach the first floor, which way are we going?"

"The main floor of the atrium will be to the left," Strasser said. "There are administrative offices to the right."

We reached the lobby level of the building and pulled open the door just enough to see what we were headed into. Soft footsteps echoed down the hall. I closed my eyes and leaned my ear to the crack in the door. Four sets. I'd have to wait until they passed before we attempted to enter the hall. There's no way I could take that many.

I closed the door as gingerly as possible, but before I could take even a half step back, it flung open, causing me to stumble backward. My gun was still in my hand so I raised it as quickly as I could, but it was too late. I was staring down the barrel end of a pistol.

"Don't move!" the soldier barked.

"Lower your weapons, team. She's one of ours." It was Carter and his team. We had found each other. My shoulders dropped in relief, and my heart rate lowered from the insane pace it had been keeping to just rapid.

"I never thought I'd be so happy to see you!" I fell against him in relief, but only for a moment when I remembered my surroundings. I collected myself and painted on a serious face. "Carter, this is Jeremy Strasser, Wren's father." I told him. "We were on our way to find you. Do you have an exit plan?"

"I can't leave without my research," Strasser declared as he stormed through Carter and his men and out into the hall.

"What the hell, newbie? Can't keep ahold of your subject?" Carter chastised. I shot him a look and chased after Strasser. Carter and his men were close behind.

"You said you destroyed all of your research," I called after him. He ignored me, and charged into another stairwell. It didn't matter how many times I called for him to stop and explain himself, he continued on his mission. At least he had the sense not to dart into the hall when he arrived on the third floor. He walked purposefully down the corridor with me on his heels. I stopped calling his name and asking him to stop. I was wasting my breath.

The walls were adorned with pictures of sciency things like cells and organisms that looked like they had come straight from my high school biology textbook. There were also pictures of distinguished looking men who were likely the administrators of this mad-scientist facility. Each gilded frame had a plaque affixed to it, identifying the person. I found Conway Harrison's portrait. He looked to be in his sixties, with salt and pepper hair. His steely eyes and the scowl on his face told me he wasn't the kind of man you wanted to make upset. But, from the tone of the email Claudia showed us, it was Moreau I should be more concerned about. Moreau seemed to call the shots. And with no picture of him to be found, I'd say he wasn't an official employee of the Regal Institute.

Doors with small, square windows lined the hall. I glanced into a few rooms as I passed, but there wasn't anything of interest until we got closer to the lab. Peering into those rooms, I saw what Strasser had warned me about. In one room, there was a man sitting on a cot. The left side of his face looked like it was melting off. He pushed at his skin, trying to put it back in place. In another room, a woman paced the floor. When she turned around and saw me, she immediately covered her face. I couldn't see what monstrous thing she hid behind her hands, but if her fused fingers were any indication, I appreciated her discretion.

I entered the lab behind Carter and watched his team move through the hall to finish rounding up everyone from scientists to executives. With its stainless steel tabletops and chemistry lab equipment, I recognized it as the room from which Strasser had recorded his message to Thatcher.

"You said you destroyed all of your research," I reminded him. "What could you possibly need from here?" Strasser pulled out a drawer and emptied the contents on to the counter. Then he lifted out the false bottom and retrieved a small box. Taking the papers out, he folded and shoved them into his pocket. "So you *didn't* destroy all the research."

"I destroyed everything associated with these horrific experiments."

"Did you do that to those people?" I pointed angrily in the direction of the rooms we had just passed. Strasser's eyes darted around the room, and then fixated on the empty box in his hand. "What did you do to them?"

Strasser hung his head for a moment before speaking. He let out a heavy sigh. "I was tasked with studying various bacteria," he said. "Evaluating the varying effects on tissue and blood samples."

"What does that mean?" Carter asked.

"Harmful bacteria that cause bacterial infections and disease are called pathogenic bacteria. Bacterial diseases occur when pathogenic bacteria get into the body and begin to reproduce and crowd out healthy bacteria, or to grow in tissues that are normally sterile. Harmful bacteria may also emit toxins that damage the body," he began explaining. "Some bacteria have the same effect on all living organisms and have a standard treatment, like strep throat and even pneumonia. Others? Others can be trickier. I was researching the others."

"Okay. So how do you get from researching bacteria to … whatever it is that's going on in those rooms?" I stumbled over my words, unsure of how to describe the things I'd never be able to erase from my mind.

"You have to understand. As researchers we are always asking 'what would happen if?' So, when they came to me and told me to find a way to alter the bacteria, I was naturally curious."

I stepped closer to him. His brow knit together in pain. He was ashamed and embarrassed.

"What did you do?"

"I … created an additive that speeds up the reproduction of the bacteria. Where a normal incubation period might be two or three weeks, these new strains can show symptoms in…" We held a collective breath. "Seventy-two hours."

"Holy. Shit." Carter's blank face said it all.

"What happens at Seventy-two hours? Is there any hope of being cured?" I begged.

"There's hope, but the longer treatment is put off, the more time the bacteria has to grow and attach itself to organs. You might have a week, maybe two, before organs start shutting down. Once that happens, it's nearly impossible to recover."

The blood drained from Strasser's face and a bolt of nervous electricity shot through me.

"They're going to infect the whole world? Even if they get billions from the world's leaders, there's no way millions of people will get the cure in time!" I exchanged terrified expressions with Carter. "How are they going to do it?"

"They're going hit every major airport around the world. Expose passengers through the ventilation systems. They will then, unknowingly, spread the bacteria to their cities," he explained.

"So, what? They breathe it in, and then every breath they exhale will infect someone else?" I asked.

"No. They won't be contagious for at least forty-eight hours. My research showed that none of the patients were contagious less than forty-eight hours from exposure. Most only became contagious once the bacteria had fully matured, closer to the seventy-two hour mark," he explained. "Some showed signs of illness at forty-eight hour mark. There were, however, some outliers."

"And what the hell were those?" Carter's question conveyed his frustration.

"Those who already had another disease."

"What happens if someone is already sick?" I was afraid of the answer.

Strasser glanced toward the door. "The people in those rooms. That's what happens."

Chapter 13

We exited the building and were greeted by the blazing sun and a team of local authorities. They piled lab employees into transport vehicles and carried them somewhere to be questioned. I suspected many of them had no idea the atrocities that were taking place there at the Regal Institute. And I wondered if the mysterious Moreau would be among them. He seemed to be the brains of the operation, and finding him would be key in stopping a global epidemic before it started.

Mercenaries from Carter's team escorted men in tailored suits from the building, wrinkling their starched shirts with less than gentle handling. I noticed Conway Harrison immediately. His scowl had turned to trepidation in the hands of a trained soldier.

"Where is she?" I shouted as I charged toward him.

"Victoria!" Carter barked, following behind me.

The soldier gripping Harrison's arm stopped him abruptly when he saw me approaching. Harrison tried to dismiss me, but the guard jerked his body, forcing him to face me.

"I don't know what you're talking about," he protested with British enunciation. He averted his eyes and set his jaw.

"Like hell you don't know what I'm talking about! Where is Wren Strasser?" I demanded. "You hired multiple bounty hunters to find her. One of them found me, kidnapped me, and brought me here. The other one posed as her boyfriend and is now holding her hostage somewhere. So where is she?"

At the mention of her name, Harrison drew his eyes back to mine. "I didn't hire anyone. But if you were smart, you'd back off. You have no idea what you're dealing with, *little girl.*"

Carter marched forward and "helped" Harrison into the transport vehicle. His hands were cuffed behind his back, and as he stepped up I caught the glimpse of a small tattoo on the inside of his wrist. It was a 3D cube, with shadowing making it look like a prism. It was no bigger than the size of a quarter and looked unsettlingly familiar.

Carter pulled me aside. "You can't let him get to you," he said reassuringly. "They all say things to try and break us down so we lose focus."

"Him belittling me is the least of my concerns right now," I said. I twisted my mouth.

"What is it?"

"Harrison has a tattoo on his wrist," I said.

"He doesn't seem the type for tattoos, but what of it?" Carter asked.

"I've seen the symbol somewhere before. Probably from a training, but I can't place it."

"I'll have them catalog it when they get him to interrogation. Then can cross-reference it with any known organizations. They'll let us know if it leads to anything. Good work, newbie." Carter smirked at me and then gave his attention to one of his men.

I found Strasser in the same place we had left him when I charged Harrison: wringing his hands as he leaned against a police car.

"We must get to Wren." Strasser's tone was desperate. "She is the only one who can protect the formula."

"We're working on finding her. But in the meantime, we can arrange for everything you need to make the antidote again," I told him

"I can't do that," Strasser rebutted.

"Why not?" Why would he refuse to make the antidote?

"It's not a cookie recipe, Miss Asher!"

"You're telling me your huge brain can't remember some formulas?" Carter countered as he approached. "You know, for a guy who wants us to save his daughter's life, you have a knack for making things very difficult."

He shot Carter a look that we've all given him at one point or another. "I can make more of the antidote, but we have to find Wren first!"

"Then just tell us where she was supposed to lead us?" Carter barked.

Strasser only shook his head and knit his brows together.

Ignoring Strasser in lieu of pummeling him, Carter stepped away while I paced in front of another police car and wondered what our next move would be. We had Strasser, but he was insistent that we find Wren before he could manufacture more of the antidote.

"Carter," Ian called. He strode toward us with determined steps. It had been a long time since I'd seen him that stone-faced and resolute. He paid no attention to me, instead making a beeline for Carter. "Give me an update."

I leaned against the car while Carter gave Ian the rundown of what had transpired since his team arrived at the Regal Institute. Strasser stood there, subjected to Ian's interrogation about who he thought had taken Wren and where the antidote was.

Suddenly I remembered the letter I had shoved in my back pocket at the bank. Strasser's note to Wren with the key told her that everything she needed to know would be in the safe deposit box, or the "treasure box" as he called it. That letter was meant to lead her to the cure.

Carter and Ian moved closer to Strasser, intimidating the distressed father into taking two steps back. I let them question him while I pulled the envelope from my pocket and tore it open. I read it, word by word, letting the information soak into my mind. My eyes grew wide as saucers as I discovered the location of the antidote.

"We're going to find Wren, Jeremy. But we need to know where the antidote is!" Ian's tone was sharp and agitated.

"Guys!" I shouted. All three men turned their attention to me. "He can't tell you where it is."

"Why not?" Ian asked tersely.

"Because he doesn't know where it is," I said. My eyes locked on Strasser's.

"What? How is that possible?" Ian questioned.

"Where did you get that?" Strasser asked frantically, pushing through the wall Ian and Carter had formed in front of him.

"In the *treasure box*. Exactly where you left it for Wren," I told him.

"But," he stuttered. "How did you know to go there?"

"She's freakishly good at figuring things out that the rest of us are blind to," Carter quipped.

"Yeah, well, I wasn't the only one who knew to go there. I was ambushed at the bank, which is how I got here," I said.

"We'll discuss that later." Ian shot me a stern look. "Does the letter say where the cure is?" he asked, guiding us back to the pressing matter of the location of the antidote.

"It does."

"Then where is it?"

"It's with Wren," I answered. "It's in her blood."

"What the fuck?" The expletive dropped like a bomb from Carter's lips.

"How on earth is the cure in Wren's bloodstream? How could you use your own daughter like that?" Ian spun around and laid into Strasser.

Strasser leaned over the car, splaying his hands on the hood. "I couldn't allow the cure to get into their hands," he began to explain. "So I did the only thing I could think to do to save it: I had it put into the ink just before Wren had her butterfly tattoo done. It's untouchable in her bloodstream."

"Who else knew about the bank in Ghent?" Ian's voice commanded. "The man I interrogated could only say that he was approached by someone with military credentials who was confident Wren would go to the safe deposit box."

Strasser darted his eyes nervously between us.

"They killed that man when we got here, so obviously he was just as duped as Booten was," I told Ian. "But the question still remains: who sent him there?" I directed my attention to Strasser. "Was it Conway Harrison?"

He shook his head. "No, no. Harrison is just as dirty as anyone in this thing, but it wasn't him."

"Was it Moreau?" Strasser's eyes widened nervously at the sound of a name he obviously thought we didn't know. "It *was* Moreau. Are you protecting him?"

He rubbed his face with his hands and let out a heavy breath. Before he could confess what he had been holding back, a ball of fire erupted in the distance. The earth shook violently, and the space around us echoed with the noise of glass shattering and crashing metal. We ducked for cover and waited until dust and debris had stopped falling around us before standing again. The convoy had been fifty yards down the road when the transport vehicle carrying Conway Harrison and his cohorts exploded. We ran toward the destruction. I expected to hear the cries and shrieks of passengers begging for help, but I didn't. The vehicle was torn into pieces, and what was left was engulfed in smoke and flames. There was no way anyone could have survived, which was the objective.

"Son of a bitch!" Carter exclaimed.

"Those were the only people who really knew what was going on!" I shouted behind him. "What do we do now?"

"Now we interrogate the hell out of Strasser. He's been holding back, and that's about to end," Ian said. "I don't care who he is to Thatcher. We need information, and he's going to give it to us."

We had just caught our breaths when we heard the roar of a helicopter. It rose above the billowing smoke from behind the Regal Institute and headed straight for us. The whirring sound of the blades was almost deafening. Dirt and smoke whirled around us, stinging my eyes. I lost sight of the others and stumbled as I tried to gain my footing in the bluster. Then I shoved my mouth and nose into the crook of my arm and ran. The helicopter flew lower and started firing at us. Bullets whizzed by, hitting metal scraps from the explosion and spitting up dirt at my feet as they barely missed me.

I found refuge behind a car, coughed, and rubbed my eyes. When I could see clearly, I looked for Strasser. He was being strong-armed by Mr. Anonymity who drove me to the compound. A woman in a silk, floral sheath dress and red patent heels followed them. The man put Strasser into the back seat of a black SUV. Before he could close the door, I fired, sending a bullet through Mr. Anonymity's head. Those days of practice with Damon's head on the target had paid off. He fell to the ground in a heap. The woman picked up his gun and attempted to run to the driver's side for a quick getaway. Her Jimmy Choos were not made for speed. I shot like a canon from where I stood and tackled her to the ground. Her gun went flying and so did my right fist. I gave a swift right hook to her jaw to make sure she knew who was in charge. She retaliated immediately and delivered an effective punch to my right cheek, splitting my skin with her ring. Still straddling her stomach, I drew my gun and pointed it at her.

I stood and kept my weapon aimed at her. "Stand up!" I commanded.

Ian and Carter ran up behind me.

"Dammit! I missed the girl fight!" Carter exclaimed.

To respond to his comment would only have encouraged him. "What happened to the helicopter?" I asked Ian. We had her outnumbered, but I was still concerned about a second round of being shot at.

"It's gone. It was obviously meant to be a distraction," he said. "Where's Strasser?"

"I'm here." Strasser approached us slowly, his eyes on the woman standing in front of me. Their eyes locked. A thousand things seemed to pass between them in that moment. And right then and there, I knew who she was.

"Oh my God," I whispered. "*You're* Moreau."

"Go ahead, Jeremy," she said flatly. Her European accent was fluid and elegant.

"Yes. This is Moreau. Natalie Moreau," he said. "Wren's mother."

Chapter 14

In the history of stunned expressions, Ian, Carter, and I had just beat all of them. Wren's own mother was behind the plan that had her kidnapped to use as bait for her father.

"You're the one behind the plan to release the bacteria." I said to her. My nostrils flared as I recalled the string of emails outlining their scheme to infect the world's population. I remembered Wren telling me that all her father would say about her mother was that she wasn't a good person. I could see where the line in their moral standards was drawn. "And you knew?" I directed my question to Strasser.

"Wren was already carrying the vaccine when I found out. Once I knew Natalia was involved, there was no doubt she would use Wren against me. Had I known earlier, I would have never involved her," he answered. He drew his attention back to his ex. "I should have known it was you."

"Wait," she replied, stunned. "You did what?" The shock on her face was real. She genuinely didn't know that Strasser had used their own daughter as a lock box for the cure.

"I did the only thing I could to keep the antidote safe," Strasser replied.

"Hold on," I said. "You've called whatever it is in Wren's bloodstream a cure, an antidote, and a vaccine. I'm no scientist, but aren't those different things?"

Strasser sighed. "Vaccines are made of dead or weakened antigens. They can't cause an infection, but the immune system still sees them as an enemy and produces antibodies in response. After the threat has passed, many of the antibodies will break down, but immune cells called memory cells remain in the body. Normally, once the memory cells have formed, the vaccine becomes part of their bloodstream. But, like the additive I created in the bacteria, I created something similar so that the vaccine can be separated from the blood, similar to the way platelets, plasma, or white blood cells can. So, technically Wren has been vaccinated, but because it can be separated from her blood, it means that she also carries the cure, or antidote, for the virus."

Natalia took two steps toward Strasser but stopped when Carter took his own step closer to her with his gun at the ready. She peered at him from the corner of her eye and dismissed him when she drew her attention back to Strasser. I wondered what was going through her mind. She seemed torn, as if she were deciding whether to hold her allegiance to the men in suits writing the checks, or to her own flesh and blood. The fact that it was even a choice was despicable.

"Let me get this straight: you injected your daughter with a cure for a disease she doesn't have so you could keep it from your ex here, who has her eyes set on world domination? You two are seriously fucked up," Carter interjected with his usual sarcasm. It shook Natalia from her introspective state and brought her attention back. Her demeanor returned to being cold and steely.

"Every relationship has its complications," she mused.

"That's not a complication. That's psychotic." I didn't hold back the contempt in my voice.

"Where is my daughter? What have you done with her?" Strasser yelled.

"Settle down, man," Carter called as he physically restrained Strasser from attacking Natalia. "We'll get the information we need out of her. Trust me."

Just then, agents in yellow hazmat suits exited the building with patients who had been used as test subjects and loaded them into ambulances that would take them to the closest hospital. They had facemasks on, keeping whatever disease was in them from being breathed into the air. After what I had already seen, I averted my eyes when they were brought out.

As they carried Stevens out, I made sure Ian knew how he had cooperated and that he didn't have a clue what they had been doing in the lab. There were also three other researchers who claimed they had no idea what had been going on in that facility for over a year. I suspected they didn't, but a full investigation would give us the truth in time.

Carter threw Natalia into the back of a car with two of his team members while he drove Strasser and me to the local police station. Ian drove separately, leaving before us. It was a silent ride. I think Strasser was still in shock to find out that Natalia wasn't just pulling the logistical strings of the operation, but that she was brazen enough to send multiple bounty hunters after her own daughter.

As the car rolled along, I thought of Ian for the first time since I sat in the back of that car with poor Mick. I had just been with him, but I hadn't put a lot of *thought* into him. I smiled. I had done it. I went to work and did my job. Ian saw me in action and had to have seen that I could come out on the other side of an assignment alive and well.

Most importantly, my performance would put Director Thatcher's concerns to rest.

When we arrived, one of Carter's men pulled Natalia out of the truck and escorted her into the station to an interrogation room. She didn't resist or even seem upset. She was obviously a sociopathic maniac bent on world domination, but even still ... something felt off.

Adam and Claudia were just inside the door when we walked in and both of them gave me high praise for my work.

"I hear you totally kicked ass in there, girl!" Claudia laughed.

"Way to go, Vic!" Adam agreed.

"Thanks, guys." I smiled. I still couldn't believe that it was me who had been thrown into such an intense situation and survived.

The main area of the police station was a large room with several desks and two hallways leading to opposite sides of the building near the back of the room. The walls were gray concrete, and the overhead lighting left a lot to be desired.

I spotted Ian across the room, his eyes locked onto mine. We met in the middle of what felt like a vast canyon of space between us. The first time we had taken any time to consider the other. Neither of us said anything at first. All the excitement and certainty that had bubbled inside me before seemed to be disappearing. The look on Ian's face made me suddenly unsure of his feelings. My heart led a pounding race inside my chest. I wondered if my disappearing right before his eyes at the bank had made him realize that being in love with me was a bad idea. I wondered if he evaluated my work on the field and found me lacking. All of a sudden I was confused. If he had second thoughts about me, would he be right?

"Carter," Ian called without taking his eyes off me. I hadn't even seen Carter come back into the room. "I need to debrief Victoria. Take lead on the interrogation. I'll be there in a moment."

"Got it!" he replied.

"Victoria, you've just completed your first mission. It's policy to debrief with your team leader," Ian said slowly.

"Okay." I echoed Ian's slow cadence and followed him as he turned from me and walked down a hall and into an office. It was just a regular office with a plain brown desk in the center. There were no papers or phone on the desk. No calendar on the wall. The room was stark and felt ominous, considering the call to the proverbial principal's office I had just received.

Ian walked in first, and I closed the door behind us. He turned and looked at me for a moment before pushing me against the wall and covering my mouth with his. His hand behind my neck kept our lips locked together and one at my waist pulled me to him. His kiss was possessive and passionate. This was the *I'm in love with you kiss* I had only just realized I wanted more than anything.

I followed suit and hooked my fingers around the belt loops of his pants and pulled. When I was satisfied that his minute step toward me had brought him as close as possible, I wrapped my arms around his waist to keep him there. Heat rose in me, making me desperate for him. I didn't want to let go ... ever.

After I had been more than sufficiently kissed, Ian pulled away and held my face in his hands.

"I'm in love with you, Ian," I said immediately. "I love you."

"I know," he said, softly brushing his lips against mine.

"What?"

"I heard you after the crash outside Bruges."

147

"Why didn't you say anything?" I replied against his mouth.

"I wanted to hear you say it when you weren't afraid I was going to die," he said.

I chuckled. "You know, I haven't thought about you since the bank."

"I'm going to need a less ego destroying explanation for that," he requested.

"I mean that when I walked into the vault, I was there to work. My mind was on what I needed to do to save Wren. And every second I was in that tunnel and with Strasser, I was focused on getting him out of there."

"You did remarkably well. But what does that have to do with us?"

"I'm a good Rogue agent, Ian. I got in there today and I thought like an agent. I was scared, but not paralyzed with fear. All the training you've been busting my ass with has actually worked. It's part of who I am now." I let out a heavy sigh. "I've been so scared that one of us would end up dead on an assignment because we were distracted by the other. I know there are no guarantees but if I, a *newbie* agent, could be thrown into the trenches and stay focused on my impromptu assignment *plus* pull off what I did today and survive … well, I can trust you to do the same. I don't need to worry about you. And you don't need to worry about me."

Ian thought for a moment, tucking a loose lock of my hair behind my ear. He brushed his fingers along my cheek and rested his hand behind my neck.

"I want to worry about you. And I want you to worry about me." Ian thought for a moment. "I never thought I'd have someone to worry about again. Never have someone to worry about me … whether I lived or died." It was hard to believe that Ian had once existed with the belief that his death would be insignificant because he had no one.

"So I guess there's no going back now. It's out there. We love each other," I said sweetly.

"Yes. It's quite out there, isn't it?" Ian kissed me again. I closed my eyes and savored every second of it, releasing the fears I had once had. "I'm sorry if I didn't make you feel safe." His eyes turned sad as he spoke.

I cupped his face with my hand to make sure I had his attention. "You do make me feel safe. And had you walked into the diner six months ago, I wouldn't have been scared at all. It's just ... I know things about this world that I never knew before; things that were plot lines to movies. I killed a man today, Ian. I don't even know what to think about that."

"That's good to hear. Not the part about killing someone. You should always have a healthy respect for life. But yours and the life of your team come first and foremost. The part about you feeling safe with me ... I have to remember that you're still so incredibly new to this world. It was perfectly normal for you to have concerns," Ian said.

"It's fine, Ian. We're here now and all is good. But, it is kind of strange, this idea of worrying about you as my guy, but not worrying about you because I know you're the most capable Rogue agent there is," I told him.

"Indeed. And you might have to cut me a little slack in the beginning here, but I promise I'm working on letting go and allowing you to be the incredible agent I know you are. I was scared out of my mind when I saw you dragged away. Booten got more than an earful from me," Ian said, his face tensing at the mention of those moments. "I have to admit it wasn't my finest hour. He took a few hits before I stopped to actually ask questions."

"I wondered what you were going to do to him. What did he tell you?" I asked.

"When he was able to speak, he told me that the man who took you told him that he was looking for the girl who would come in and want access to box forty-five. He told Booten you were in grave danger," Ian explained.

"His name was Mick. I don't know if he ever knew what was really going on, but another guy said there had been a bounty on Wren. Natalia could have easily known about the safe deposit box and figured it was just as good as any a place to look for her once both Char and the make-out team from Oxford failed to deliver her," I thought aloud.

"Sounds like she didn't get a check-in from Char until after Mick got you," he said.

I took a deep breath and looked around the room to remind us that we were standing in an empty office in a Belgian police station, and that we had a subject in the interrogation room with Carter. It was time to get back to the task at hand. "How do you plan on getting Wren's whereabouts from Natalia?" I wondered if Ian would use the same tactic on Natalia as he did on Booten.

"Right," Ian replied. "Carter's got a good start on her, so let's see where he is."

Chapter 15

"You're not going to get anything from her," Strasser said as he rubbed his forehead in disappointment. "She's a steel trap. Believe me, I should know."

We watched Carter for a few minutes through the two-way glass as he circled Natalia, intimidating her with his height and stature. Meanwhile, Claudia was busy at a computer hacking back into the lab's entire system. She searched the emails between Natalia and Conway Harrison, and then every high-ranking administrator to the lowliest of employees, looking for any correspondence that might contain even the smallest of clues. Nothing stood out at all.

I looked at Strasser then looked back at Natalia, the wheels in my head beginning to turn rapidly.

"Pull Carter out of there," I told Ian. He looked at me for only a moment before he knocked on the window, indicating to Carter that he was needed on our side of the glass.

"I hope someone in here has a better plan. She's not budging, and all I want to do is knock that smug look off her face," Carter said as soon as he entered the room.

"Don't look at me," Ian said. "I'm just following her orders." He looked at me and nodded. Then they *all* looked at me and I realized that I may have been a bit overzealous.

"I need you to come in there with me," I said to Strasser. I expected Ian to stop me before I got started, but all I got was a slight twist of his head while he waited to see what I was going to do.

"What?" Confusion covered Strasser's face.

"I need to get inside Natalia's head. She's strong and we're not going to break her on our own," I told him.

"What makes you think I'll be able to do anything?"

"Because she still has feelings for you," I said matter-of-factly. "I saw the way she looked at you. She could have picked anyone to create that cure, but she chose you. And when you told her Wren was carrying the cure? That was genuine shock. It's become personal for her." Strasser didn't respond except to shut his eyes and clench his jaw. It seemed the anger and bitterness of the life he used to have with Natalia still hung heavy on his heart. "We're losing precious time."

Strasser let out a concerned breath. "Okay."

I opened the door to the interrogation room. Natalia's ramrod back and pointed chin didn't shift even a millimeter. But when Jeremy Strasser walked in behind me, that changed. Her breathing became shallow. She uncrossed and crossed her legs twice. She swallowed hard. And, just for a moment, her perfectly postured shoulders curved.

"Have a seat," I instructed Strasser. Now it was my turn for nerves to rocket through me. I took a cleansing breath and reminded myself that my gut had never lied to me and to go with what it seemed to be screaming.

"Jeremy," I began. I hadn't used his first name before but had to set a personal tone. "I'm curious. Can you tell me how you and Natalia met?"

"Really?" she scoffed. "Well, at least you're not wasting time asking me questions you know I won't answer."

Strasser's concerned eyes darted up at me. I telepathically told him to trust me, and hoped my eyes conveyed that to him. I nodded for him to go ahead and answer.

"Well, um … we met when I was still in the Army. I was stationed here in Brussels, and she was a researcher fresh out of medical school. The Army contracted with their department on a partnership doing research on a psychotropic drug treatment for PTSD. We had the same dreams of changing the world through science and winning Nobel prizes. We fell for each other immediately, and within six months she had moved into my apartment. We were very much in love. Everything about us was perfect."

"Of course you thought it was perfect," she scoffed. Her stiff body language said she was pissed, but her eyes and the softness of her face told me that seeing Jeremy touched her hardened heart, even if in the smallest way.

"It *was* perfect … for a time," he said softly. He paused as he recollected their story. "We were together two years when you started to change. You worked longer hours, cutting yourself off from me. I thought it was the marriage thing. We had talked a lot about getting married but it never seemed like the right time. But I bit the bullet and proposed over lunch one day." Strasser looked up at me. "It wasn't as momentous an occasion as I thought it would be. Most women get all emotional about that sort of thing … not Natalia. She kissed me, said yes, I put the ring on her finger, and we both went back to work."

I circled the table, walking behind each of them. Natalia hadn't moved in her seat. She watched Strasser speak at first, but then gave her attention to her hands. She fidgeted with them a lot, rolling them around each other as if she was washing them.

"When Wren was a kid, you told her that her mother was *not a good person*, which we all know is adult speak for 'your mother is bat-shit crazy.' So what happened?" When he didn't reply right away, I gave my attention to Natalia. The two held each other's gaze. There were so many stories to be told and not enough time to tell them. But a gaze like that could only be rooted in one thing: love.

"What happened when she got pregnant?" I asked him. The question didn't break the lock their eyes had on one another. Natalia did that when she turned her chin to her shoulder.

"She wasn't overjoyed," he began quietly. "She wanted to end the pregnancy, but I convinced her it was going to be wonderful. Nothing I said made much of a difference. I was still the only one talking baby names and nursery designs. I thought finding out we were having a girl might spark something inside her, but she remained little more than uninterested.

"I got the safe deposit box so we could start putting special things away for Wren. You know, family heirlooms and such. I thought it might do something for Natalia to connect our family lineage to our baby. I basically spent my time grasping at straws."

Strasser ran his hand across his scalp and leaned back in his chair completely deflated.

"After Wren was born, we could both stay home for six weeks, but Natalia went back after three. She was itching to get back to work. She didn't want to breast feed and barely held Wren. She worked longer hours than before she was pregnant.

"When Wren was six months old, Natalia came home with wide, happy eyes. I didn't know what had happened and I didn't care. The woman I had fallen in love with seemed to be back. We … were together that night for the first time since long before Wren was born. It was … wonderful."

"As we lay there together, she told me why she was so happy. She had been offered a job by a biomedical firm in Germany. The more she explained the job, the more it was clear it involved some very sketchy ethical practices. She said that it was important to the future of science. When I told her I couldn't condone that, she told me how much they were going to pay her, thinking that seven figures would somehow make me change my mind.

"We went to sleep and in the morning we kept to our normal routines. I got up with Wren as usual while Natalia got ready for work. She breezed through the kitchen as she normally did, gave us each a kiss on the cheek, and left. I put Wren in her playpen and went into the bathroom. That's when I saw it. She left her engagement ring on the counter." Strasser sighed. "She had already accepted the job in Germany. I saw her twice before she moved. Today is the first time I've seen her since then."

Natalia finally looked up at Jeremy. The tip of her nose was red and her eyes were glassy. She was working hard to not let her emotions show. It made me wonder where the switch got flipped. What mattered most was that Natalia was breaking. My next move was the only one I had. I was running on instinct and hoping for results. I mentally crossed my fingers and left the room.

Strasser had been the last person Natalia expected to walk through the door with me. Her eyes widened just a bit and the corners of her mouth lifted ever so slightly when she saw him. When he began to speak, she couldn't take her eyes off him. It was only when he spoke of her pregnancy that she had to look away.

"Did you see that?" I said as I entered the observation room. "She had physical reaction to seeing him."

Carter moved from his place by the wall and joined Ian and me closer to the window.

"She seems like the same stone cold bitch here that she was at the lab," Carter said. We watched the former lovers through the two-way glass. Strasser stood and paced the room while Natalia took slow, deep breaths.

Strasser stood and Natalia's eyes shifted slightly in his direction before she smoothed the skirt of her dress under the table and crossed her legs.

"See that?" I pointed out.

"See what?" Carter questioned.

"It's like poker. These are her tells. The way she checks to see if he's looking. The way she straightens her dress."

Carter furrowed his brow and adjusted the volume up on the speaker next to the window, and the three of us listened while we watched the.

"Jeremy," she said softly. "Why don't you sit back down?"

He walked the length of the room before answering. "I'd rather stand."

Natalia looked down at her hands and threaded them together.

"I'm the last person you ever wanted to see again, so I'm assuming they forced you to come in here," she said.

"That wasn't always the case." He turned to her, letting his eyes finally take her in. "There was a time I would have given anything for you to come back to us."

Natalia was taken aback. Surprise painted her face. After a moment she pushed herself away from the table, straightening her dress as she stood. I elbowed Carter. "See." She crossed the room and examined herself in the mirror of her side of the window at an awkwardly close range.

"I couldn't come back. You changed." Natalia used her pinky finger to clear the lipstick from the corners of her mouth.

"How can you say that?" His challenge whipped Natalia around. She took three determined steps toward him, stopping just before her proximity to him became uncomfortable. He reached up and gently touched the swelling knot I had put on her jaw. Strasser shook his head, walked past her to the table, and gripped the chair with white-knuckle force.

"You stopped caring about changing the world with science. You were more concerned with your boring lab position at that hospital, looking at biopsies all day," she bemoaned. "You were made for more than that, and you know it!" Natalia's emotional response to Strasser was more than I could have hoped for. "But you got scared, and then you got comfortable. When we got together, we both wanted to forge a new frontier in medicine."

Strasser closed the distance between them. "It's you who changed! You decided that forging a new frontier meant ignoring the ethics of medical research, and I disapproved of that," he countered. "Isn't that why you left me? Why you left Wren?"

Natalia stepped even closer into Strasser's personal space with an angry force. "You made it perfectly clear she was *your* daughter when you kicked me out!"

I looked at Ian and Carter and saw that their jaws were as slack as mine. Natalia was telling a different story than

Strasser had laid out only a few minutes ago. A story where Natalia wasn't altogether to blame for the destruction of their relationship.

"What are you talking about? I didn't kick you out," Strasser moved back, rubbing his forehead and the back of his neck while avoiding eye contact with his ex.

Natalia furrowed her brow. "You can't honestly tell me you think that fairytale of a story you just told is how it happened." She cocked her head and tried to catch his eyes, but he continued to avert them. "I told you there was a position for you with the company in Germany, as well. You said I was out of my mind if I thought you were going to take *your* daughter to Germany and work for an 'unethical' biomedical firm. You also told me that you had had enough and that I could go if I wanted to. That you were washing your hands of me."

"Washing his hands of her," I thought out loud.

"Why is that important?" Carter asked.

"Did you see how she was fidgeting with her hands earlier? Rolling them around like she was washing them? If that's one of the last things he said before kicking her to the curb, well… Having come face to face with him is bringing all that pain back up."

"Talk about a woman scorned," Carter quipped.

"My mother always said that a woman betrayed never forgets."

"I was angry. I didn't actually think you would leave." Distress covered Strasser's face as he spoke. It seemed he was just realizing that he was more responsible for Natalia's departure than he once believed.

"It's fine, Jeremy," she said stoically. She turned away and took a few steps toward the table, straightening her dress again, although it hadn't been disturbed since she stood. "I washed my hands of you that day, too."

"Why didn't you say something? Anything? We had a good life together, Natalia. I know it wasn't much, but we had a family and a good home." He reached for her hand in what could only be seen as a moment of weakness. The young man who had fallen in love with Natalia was fighting for her. It wouldn't be long before the man Strasser had become would take over.

She pulled her hand away before Strasser could touch it and folded her arms in front of her defiantly. "You're the one who wanted a family. And that place you called a home was barely livable. It still is."

Strasser's face turned crimson. "So you're getting back at me by endangering our daughter?"

"If not for your genius plan of keeping the vaccine alive in her blood, she wouldn't be in this predicament." She raised her voice and then brought it back down to her menacing tone. "The plan doesn't work without the cure. God knows I don't want half of my face falling off. And now that we know where the cure is, we can continue moving forward. We'll have the antidote in a matter of hours. That sweet boy she's been seeing was kind enough to transport her to a location where we'll be able to extract the cure from her. She *probably* won't die in the process."

"You're lying! There's no way they could know Wren holds the cure!"

"Are you sure?" Natalia turned and sauntered toward the two-way mirror. "What was his name? Ah, yes. Carter. He might want to employ a more thorough vetting system for the contracted muscle."

Carter's eyes widened, putting two and two together: one of his men had been a mole. He spun on his heels and flung the observation room door open, shouting for someone named Miller in the process.

Terror spread across Strasser's face. "I could believe that you wouldn't waste a second before putting a bullet in my head, but I can't believe you would kill our daughter!" Strasser snarled in disgust.

"I resent that, Jeremy. Just because I never wanted to be a mother doesn't mean I don't value my daughter's life," she said in her defense. "I said she *probably* won't die. I mean … unless they draw too much blood at once." She teased Strasser with her sinister tone.

Strasser lunged at Natalia. His fingers dug into her arms with a force that immediately turned them bright red. He shook her twice as he yelled.

"Where is my daughter? Where did you take her? I swear to God I'll kill you if I lose her!" he shouted repeatedly as he shook her again.

Ian darted into the interrogation room and pulled Strasser off Natalia. I followed close behind. Strasser begged Natalia to tell him where Wren was and only stopped once Carter arrived. He fell into a chair and put his face in his hands and wept.

"You think this begins and ends with me?" she laughed. "This goes so much deeper than you could ever imagine!" The cold, heartless bitch was back.

"You're going to draw her blood? Well at least we know she's in a hospital, or at least a clinic." I looked at Strasser reassuringly. Claudia should be able to easily find Wren if she was having a medical procedure done, even if it were being done covertly. Someone is always willing to talk.

"Something like that." Natalia's cryptic reply sent Strasser over the edge. He charged at her over the table, causing Natalia to step and stumble backward. I was tempted not to catch her, but the better angels of my nature kicked in and made sure her beautiful dress never made contact with the dusty floor. While I had her, I kept her, twisting one arm behind her.

Ian exited the room for all of four seconds and returned with two uniformed officers. He said something to them in French, and they escorted her from the room.

"What the hell is going on around here?" Carter's frustrated words echoed in the small room. "Miller had Natalia and went AWOL after he deposited her."

"Why not just take her?" I wondered.

"Too many eyes. Easier to give him information and have him execute the plan than to try and escape with her," Carter explained.

I watched Strasser's shoulders shake and listened to his muffled tears from behind his hands. He was so broken and afraid. I understood his pain and worry. Not knowing whether the only family you have left is safe or not is terrifying.

"She'll never tell us where Wren is," Strasser bemoaned.

"She already did," I said.

Strasser looked up with confusion while Ian and Carter waited for my explanation.

"She said the home you shared was barely livable. Then she said *it still is*. How would she know the condition of that building today unless she had been there?" I told them.

"Seems like a crazy place to perform a medical procedure, even one as simple as drawing blood," Carter offered.

"She's probably just using it as a holding platform," Ian said reassuringly. "But at this point I wouldn't put anything past her."

"They don't really need to draw *a lot* of blood, do they?" I asked warily. Time was of the essence, and I was concerned we were quickly running out of it.

Strasser stood and wiped the moisture from his face. "Not necessarily," he answered. "But I don't know how many doses of the cure they're trying to create. You can only extract so much from a blood sample before you need another one. I do know that Natalia's right. That building should be condemned. Even with the right medical equipment, it would be terribly dangerous to perform any procedure there."

"We're going to find her," Ian said. He put his hand on Strasser's shoulder. "I promise."

"Ian," Carter began.

Ian shook his head once and then poked his head outside the interrogation room door. He asked someone about helping Strasser get a cup of coffee. A kind looking older woman came to the door and escorted Strasser out.

Carter continued his thought. "You can't make promises like that, man."

"Yeah, well … I just did."

"What's the next move?" I asked before Carter could rebut.

Ian looked at me and then walked into the main area of the station. It was a busy place, with police officers moving around the room, answering calls, and seeing to a few citizens who had come in since we had arrived and disturbed their day. The rest of Carter's team had gathered to one side of the room while they awaited further instructions. Those instructions turned out to be a dismissal. The men exited the station without question.

Ian found the police captain and spoke to him in short, direct sentences. As he walked back toward us, Ian made a call on his cell.

"Perfect," he said just before he ended the call. "Claudia is pulling up the location of the apartment. Carter, you'll lead your team in and search it from top to bottom," Ian instructed as he rolled a sleeve that had fallen.

"I'm calling in my own team for the rest of this mission," he told Ian.

"Makes sense to me," Ian replied.

"If she's there, we'll find her." Carter nodded and left. He got on his cell and began barking orders to someone. I felt confident that whoever he brought in would more than exceed his high standards.

Ian checked his phone, and I waited for him to give me my instructions. When he became engrossed in the information he was receiving, I prompted him.

"What do we need to do before we meet up with Carter and his team?" I asked.

Ian looked up from his phone, making only momentary contact with my eyes before he looked back down. I knew exactly what his silence was telling me.

"Don't do this to me, Ian."

He put his phone in his pocket and gave me the attention my tone was demanding.

"You've just been through a traumatic experience, Victoria, and I feel—"

"Bullshit." I crossed my arms and bore my eyes into his. "What happened to 'working on it'? This is keeping me grounded because you're scared."

Ian closed his eyes and bowed his head. "You're right," he said softly as he looked up at me. "My nervousness about you being out there has nothing to do with your abilities. You've more than proven yourself."

I took Ian's hand in mine. "I am always going to do everything I can to get back to you." I leaned up on my toes and kissed him sweetly. "We're a team. I don't want to do this without you. Please don't make me." He knew I was serious.

As if a switch flipped in him, Ian straightened his back and pulled out his phone. He tapped and swiped and paused as he reviewed the information on the screen. Then he typed something and put the phone back in his pocket.

"All right," he said. "Carter's team is en route to the Strassers' old flat building. Claudia is uploading the schematics for the building to all of us. It's about thirty minutes from here, so we'll review it in the car."

"Great. Let's go."

Chapter 16

I pulled up the blueprints for the apartment building as soon as we got into the car. Ian drove fast and asked for my feedback just as quickly.

"What do you see?" he asked.

"Nothing out of the ordinary. There are two entrances, one on the main street and another on the back alley. Four floors and a basement." I pointed to a small square on the south side of the building. "This looks like it could be a way in and out of the basement. But unless it has some hidden passages like the bank did, it looks like a normal apartment building."

Ian concentrated on the road as he spoke. "Based on the information Claudia has, there are no underground tunnels leading to or from this building. The areas you've noted are the only ways in and out."

When we arrived at the meeting point, about half a block from the building, Carter was using a scrap piece of wood to draw a crude rendition of the layout for the building in the dirt. His new team of six men was huddled around him in the amber glow of the setting sun.

"Team one will enter this side through the main entrance and start with the first floor. Team two, you'll take the west side and work your way down from the fourth." Carter gave Ian and me his attention as he continued instructing his team. "Hale, Asher, and I will hit the basement."

"Keep your ears on and maintain a light step. Take out whoever you need to in order to find the girl," Ian added.

"You heard the man. Let's move." Carter pulled an earpiece from his front shirt pocket and placed it in his ear. His team followed suit. Ian handed me the same small device and I put it in my ear. In an instant, I was hearing chatter from each person on the team as they spoke.

I followed behind Carter and Ian through the back entrance of the building and down the stairs that led into the basement. Rather than a hall in the center and rooms on either side like the floors above us, there was one path to the far right and huge rooms to the left. It seemed at one time it might have been a storage location for residents. Whatever it was then, it was a dark and dungeon-like place now. The ceiling hung low and stunk of mold and urine. My gag reflex kicked in more than once.

Strong voices rang through our ears as each team checked in.

"Team two: clear."

"Team three: clear."

"That leaves just us," I said in a hushed tone. We had checked two small rooms and found nothing but empty barrels and a few stacks of boxes. The third room was another story. Slumped in the corner with a bullet hole in his head was Char. I sighed. "Oh, Char."

"Looks like they had no intention of paying any of the bounty hunters they sent after Wren," Ian commented. "We'll send for an ambulance when we're done here. Hopefully we'll only need one."

Leaving Char's body, we continued our search for Wren. We maneuvered down the long corridor with guns raised. Entering the final room, we let out a collective, "What the hell?" Before us was a makeshift space marked by four sheets of plastic hanging from the ceiling to create a room within the room. The tarps were frosted, but we could see that no one was behind them.

We pushed the tarp aside like a shower curtain and entered the space. Inside was a long, metal table with four brown straps attached to it: two at the foot and two at what would be wrist level. I shuddered. The medical equipment was sparse.

"Dammit!" Ian turned over a small metal cart as more expletives left his lips.

"It's okay, Ian. We'll go back to Natalia and—"

"You think she's just going to tell us where they've taken her ... if she's even still alive? We're only here because we followed *your* hunch!" Ian's nostrils flared and his eyes were almost bulging. I stepped back in an attempt to give him some room to breathe. Although his implication that I had done something wrong made me want to give Ian a piece of my mind.

"It's not Vic's fault we're too late, so calm the hell down, man!" Carter said in my defense.

Ian put his hands on his hips and turned around, taking in four solid breaths before returning to the moment.

I surveyed the room and considered what had gone down in there. *Poor Wren*, I thought.

Wait.

"This is all a set up," I declared.

"What makes you think that?" Ian asked.

I stepped next to the bed. "There's not even a table for tools and supplies. They'd want to draw the blood and begin separating it right away. Why draw the blood here if they had to transport it somewhere else? At most, they drugged her up here so they could take her somewhere else." I said.

I had barely explained my theory when I thought my eardrum was going to explode from the shouts ringing through our earpieces.

"Team one! Team one!" a voice shouted. "Team two has been ambushed!" Gunfire and thuds like bricks sounded above us. We spun around and headed for the door.

"I've got the east stairwell. You take the west!" Carter didn't look back as he raced to the aid of his team.

"Stay here, Victoria," Ian barked.

"What? No!"

His eyes bore into mine. "I need your *eyes* in here."

I opened my mouth to argue, but Ian cut me off faster than I could breathe.

"I won't argue with you, Victoria. Stay. Here." Ian charged through the door and up to meet the rest of the team but not without one final directive. "Stay alert!"

I blew out a hard rush of frustrated air. I tried to be angry, but concern took its place. More thuds and crashes pounded on the ceiling, sending dust sprinkling down on me. I watched the dirty snow begin to rain down along the other side of the room as the fighting above moved down the hall. I said a silent prayer, swatted the particles away from my face, and turned back to the scene I was tasked with exploring. That's why I was here: for my eyes, not for my tactical skills, although I was a damn good shot.

I surveyed the scene. My heart ached for what Wren went through in that cold, sterile place. The fear that must have raged through her. Did they question her relentlessly? And what did they do when she couldn't give them the answers they demanded? Tears welled up in my eyes as I envisioned her crying out for her father as she was strapped down and a needle shoved into her arm to, at the very least, sedate her, or possibly take a sample of blood to confirm that she indeed did carry the antidote.

I shook my head and blinked my eyes until the tears dried up. Before me was a simple set up. One table for Wren and another that looked like a small serving tray, likely used for small medical tools. There was a folding chair next to the cart Ian had overturned and a small trashcan next to it.

I eyed the trash. Would they be dumb enough to leave a clue in plain sight? Your average psychopathic killer set on world domination wasn't likely to be trained to draw blood. The suckers they got to do it would have been in automatic mode and tossed things as they were rushed through the procedure. I squatted down next to the can, tipped it over, and began to rummage. Paper, packaging, and wadded up surgical tape filled the bin, along with a few sterile gauze pads with tinges of blood. We could have the blood tested, but that seemed a waste of time. We knew whose it was. As I pulled items out from the bottom, I unearthed a balled-up piece of yellow lined paper, like the kind from a legal pad. I opened the paper and smoothed it out on the floor.

The clock is ticking, Victoria.

I fell on to my backside in shock. Whoever planted that note knew *I* would be the one looking for clues. That meant they knew me, or at least knew enough about me. That list was relatively short, and monumentally frightening. Sadly, my own team was on the list, followed by Director Thatcher. But in bright, bold letters at the top was one name: Damon Pazzia. Natalia said this operation went deeper than we could imagine. Who else would leave a note specifically for me? It was meant to taunt me as only Damon could.

The fighting on the floor above me had stopped. I wondered if Ian and Carter had chased the culprits outside, or if they had defeated them altogether. Footsteps echoed in the hall outside as Ian and Carter made their way back to me. I folded the paper haphazardly and shoved it in my back pocket. Before I showed it to Ian, I had to follow up with Claudia and connect the dots between Damon and Natalia. This was the break I had hoped for in my quest to avenge my brother.

The steps in the hall got closer. Initially, I assumed it was Ian and Carter returning from the ass kicking they had been giving, but the sound was off. They both wore military type boots. The shoes moving toward me were some kind of sneaker, and the wearer shuffled one foot as he walked. More importantly, there was only one person headed my way.

I gave the container one last look and made sure my gun was ready. "Nothing here," I said as I stood. I whipped my gun up swiftly and pointed it at the man standing before me in scrubs and a lab coat. "Freeze," I instructed. It wasn't as commanding as I had practiced in the mirror, but at least Carter wasn't there to point out how weak I sounded.

Eyes wide, the man turned on his heels and sped down the hall. I fired once, and splinters exploded from the doorframe. I followed him out into the hall in time to see him enter the stairwell. By the time I reached the stairs, he was already a flight ahead. I fired at him again, and this time the bullet dinged off the metal railing. "Dammit!"

I took the stairs two at a time and followed him up and outside, then down a street to the left of the building. He was fast. The distance between us grew. I increased my pace and my lungs began to burn. I pumped my arms, the weight of my gun giving me an extra workout. He looked back a few times with a sinister smile spread across his face.

"Victoria," Ian's voice said sternly through my earpiece. "Where are you?"

Crap.

It wasn't until then that I thought to press the button on my earpiece.

"Um…." I stuttered as I ran.

"Are you panting?" he asked.

I took four seconds to contemplate what I was going to say. Ian was sure to be furious that I took off without a single word, especially after he ordered me to stay put.

What the hell. He's already pissed!

"I've got one! He bolted out the west side door," I said breathlessly. "Take the first street to the left."

"Bloody hell, Victoria!"

Yep. He's pissed.

"Stay put! We're coming." Ian declared.

I couldn't stay put. Someone with answers we desperately needed was getting away, and I couldn't let that happen.

The man disappeared down an alley. I ran faster, afraid he would enter one of the buildings and then I'd never find him. I rounded the corner and was immediately clotheslined across the chest. My bones rattled as I landed hard on my back. When my hand slammed to the ground, my gun flew from my grip and rocketed under a parked car. In a flash he was over me, grabbing and lifting me by my jacket. As I struggled to gain my footing, he released one hand long enough to backhand me across the face. I tasted blood. That's when I jabbed my knee into his crotch. He released me and doubled over, so I kneed him in the face, too.

I dove to the ground and went for my gun. My arm stretched as far as it could under the car, and I willed my fingers to be a quarter-inch longer. I almost had it when two fists grasped my ankles and dragged me across the pavement. I flipped over, pressed my feet into his chest, and shoved as hard as I could. He was strong and heavy, laying his weight against me, but I managed to push hard enough to make him stumble back. I didn't have time to go for my gun again, so I jumped to my feet and tried to recall every hand-to-hand combat technique Ian and Adam taught me, as well as a few from my trusty YouTube videos.

First, I knuckled him in the throat. He choked and coughed right before he rammed into me like linebacker, crashing us into a car. When he came at me again, I slid to the side and used his own force to smash his head into the car window. Thinking I bought enough time, I went for my gun again. Mistake. He grabbed me from behind, his arm across my chest. I lifted my knees to my chest and shoved off of the car door. He stumbled back and fell to the ground, allowing me to roll backward and out of his grasp. Before he could stand, I jabbed my foot into this nose. When he reached for his face, I gave him one more jolt to the crotch for good measure. Blood poured from his nose as he writhed in pain on the asphalt.

I dropped next to the car, slid a leg under the body where my gun was hiding, and kicked it closer. Gun in hand, I stood over my assailant with the barrel pointed at him. I was about to question him when Ian's voice barked in my ear.

"Victoria! Where are you?" His anger hadn't dissipated.

I pressed my earpiece. "I'm in an alley about sixty yards off the first street I followed him down. On the right," I told him. With my gun still pointed at my opponent, I waited for my tongue lashing from Ian. My heart raced with excitement. I couldn't wait for Ian to see how I had handled myself.

"You'll regret this," the man said, rasping in an English accent, as he rose to his knees and then to his feet.

"The only thing I regret is how difficult I've made it for you to speak. You have a lot of questions to answer," I told him. "Now put your hands behind your head." I finally had a chance to examine my attacker. To describe him as taller than me was unnecessary, as everyone but small children are taller than me. He had typical features, nothing that set him apart from any average-looking guy. But with his hands behind his head, his arms were now exposed. He had a single tattoo on the inside of his forearm. It was exactly like the one I had seen earlier. The shading and design were so realistic that it appeared to almost jump off of his skin.

"Vic!" Carter's voice echoed off the buildings towering around us.

"It's too late," my opponent muttered. "It's too late for all of us. The clock is ticking."

My brows knit together. "What did you say?"

The words had just left my lips when I was grabbed from behind. My assailant pulled my elbows together behind my back and snatched my gun from me. My head turned enough to see that it was another man, and it appeared that he was wearing scrubs just like the man lying on the ground in front of me. I tried to break free, but his hold on me was strong. I heard a small popping sound and then the scratch of something sharp against my neck.

"NO!" Ian screamed as he and Carter finally found me.

"It's too late," the voice behind me warned. "It's too late for all of us." The next thing I felt was the sting of a needle piercing my skin and the rush of fluid emptying into my neck.

Chapter 17

As quickly as the man grabbed me, he let go and ran in the opposite direction down the alley. He took maybe five steps before Ian shot him dead. I dropped to my knees and pressed my hand against my neck. The puncture wound was sore and tender to the touch. My mind raced and reviewed everything that had transpired from finding the note in the trash to being ambushed. I cataloged everything I had done right and everything I had done wrong. Unfortunately, the wrong was all that mattered.

Ian sprinted to me while Carter handled the guy I had chased into that alley. Two cars pulled up and two of Carter's new team members got out of each. They dragged my assailant over to the first car and shoved him in the back seat, and then waited for further instruction.

Ian knelt next to me and examined my wound.

"I'm sorry, Ian! I'm so sorry!" I cried. "You told me never to assume there was only one subject. I left myself open and now…"

"Shh," he admonished. "That's not important right now. Right now, I need you to calm down and be pragmatic." He took my face in his hands and concentrated on me. He breathed in and out slowly. I mimicked him, bringing my heart rate back to a human pace.

I nodded when I knew I could do what he asked. "I have seventy-two hours," I said flatly.

"What do you mean you have seventy-two hours?" Confusion covered Ian's face.

"He doesn't know?" I turned to Carter and asked.

"We haven't debriefed that far," he answered. "We've been focused on finding the girl."

"Which one of you is going to tell me what seventy-two hours means?" Ian was angry now.

I looked at Carter. I'd never seen a more desperately sad look on his face. He knew what I had to tell Ian and knew it was going to crush him.

"The bacteria that I was just injected with has been modified." I spoke slowly. "Strasser created and altered a deadly bacteria with an additive that accelerated the incubation period from weeks to seventy-two hours."

It took a moment for Ian to respond. He stood and brought me with him. "Then we'll just get Strasser to develop the antidote without his daughter."

"We already tried, remember," Carter said. For the first time, I watched Ian become rattled. "But here's what we are going to do," he continued. "We're going to get Vic to a hospital and have her quarantined."

"No!" I protested. "Strasser said that patients had forty-eight hours before they were contagious. There's no way I'm walking away from this to become the girl in the bubble!"

Carter's tone softened along with his expression. "We already almost lost you once. We're not going through that again." Ian cast his gaze on Carter.

I gripped Carter's hand and squeezed it gently. No matter how big of a jerk he could be to me, he really cared.

In fact, my relationship with Carter had begun to remind me of Gil. And, oddly enough, that brought me more comfort than I would have ever thought it could.

"Then let me do my job. We'll find the cure, and everything will be fine." I wasn't sure which one of us I was trying to convince. Either way, backing down now would only make things worse for me. I had to be out there. I had to be searching for Wren. And I had to figure out who left that note for me in the trash.

We arrived at the local hospital where Strasser had been sequestered. Regardless of not having his notes, he was ordered to begin working toward finding the cure again. Now that I had been infected, he would have samples to work with. So, first things being first, Strasser drew my blood and filled six vials. We had commandeered space in the basement. It was creepy on so many levels, but primarily because this is where the morgue was. Strasser worked on one side of the room while we spread out all the intel Claudia had gathered.

"Where's Adam?" I asked. "Shouldn't he be here?"

"He's interrogating your friend from the alley," Ian explained. "He'll join us later." He dipped his chin to Claudia.

"No one involved has any record of being associated with any terrorist organization or mob. Conway Harrison has nothing but glowing accolades from every nationally and globally recognized medical research organization. And Natalie Moreau is barely a blip on the radar. The most I can find on everyone else from the Regal Institute is an employment record. None of them even has a parking ticket. I can't figure out how on earth they were chosen," Claudia told us. She clacked away at her laptop. "I have run them through every database and facial recognition program out there. There's nothing, and that pisses me off."

"What about this?" I pulled a legal pad over and began drawing. It was a crude representation, but it was darn close to the tattoo on Harrison and the punk in the alley.

"What is that?" Ian picked up the pad and examined my drawing.

"It's the tattoo I saw on Conway Harrison's wrist, and the guy in the alley had the same one," I told him. "I know I've seen it somewhere before, but I can't place it. I was sure it was something you had shown me in training. But by the look on your face, you don't have a clue either."

"I don't recall seeing this, but that doesn't mean it isn't in the catalog I had you study. If it's part of an organized group, they've been dormant for quite a while. Claudia?" He handed the paper to her. She studied it and shook her head.

"I'm at a loss, too, but give me a few minutes to see if the system comes up with anything," she said. Claudia entered search criteria into the database she was using and got to work. I crossed the room to check on Strasser. He was looking under the microscope and feverishly jotting down notes.

"You look worried," I said to him. "That's not a good sign, is it?"

He stared at me for a moment. "Actually, I'm quite relieved now."

"So you think you can recreate the cure?"

"I'm hopeful, but that's not what has me relieved. I thought I saw an abnormality in your blood. I was concerned you may have been sick but didn't know it. You saw what the bacteria did to those people." He hung his head. "I'm so sorry, Victoria."

"Hey," I said. I put my hand on his shoulder. "It's going to be fine. I know you'll find the cure again."

"And I know you'll find my daughter."

"Sounds like we're both going to do everything we can not to let the other down." I gave him a tightlipped smile.

"Be honest: do you think she's still alive?" he asked. His voice trembled, probably having contemplated whether he should ask that question or not.

I sighed. "They need her for the cure," I answered. I refrained from adding the truth, which was that they'd likely kill her after they extracted it from her. The fact that her mother was involved didn't necessarily mean that she'd be spared. "Don't worry. We're going to find her."

I joined Ian and Carter as they discussed the pros and cons of interrogating Natalie Moreau further. Carter looked at me a few times, but Ian remained focused on his conversation and a file he flipped through four times before Carter brought the conversation to me.

"What do you think, newbie?" he asked.

"Well—" I began.

"Victoria doesn't have interrogation experience. Her opinion on the subject is irrelevant."

"Okay then," Carter said. "While you're being a dick, I'm going to see what Claudia's got."

Carter winked at me as he walked away. I sat on a stool next to the table and waited to see if Ian was going to apologize or offer some kind of explanation for his rude response. When he didn't, I spoke up.

"Are you still mad at me about the second subject in the alley? I said I was sorry, Ian." I took the file from him and set it behind me.

"May I have the file back, please?" he asked with no emotion.

"No. Not until you tell me why you're being a jerk," I demanded. I raised my voice, causing the others to turn their attention to us. Ian looked at them, and then looked at me. Then he left the room.

I rolled my eyes, stood up, and followed him.

"*Now* will you tell me why you've barely said three words to me since we got here, and why the ones you have spoken have put you in the running for douchebag of the year?" I crossed my arms and waited for him to respond.

His nostrils flared and his breath deepened. He rubbed his chin and twisted his mouth, all as he contemplated what he was going to say.

"I told you to stay in the basement. You deliberately disobeyed my orders," he said firmly.

"I'm sorry about that, but if I didn't follow him, we wouldn't have that guy in custody," I said in my defense.

"You also wouldn't be infected with a deadly bacteria and days away from dying."

I drew in a breath of realization. "This isn't about me disobeying orders. This is about being faced with the reality of my mortality," I said softly. "We can't keep doing this, Ian. It's literally my first assignment and you've already freaked out on me twice. Now, I love you, but if this is how it's going to be every time I'm in danger…"

"All right, before I may have gotten a little over protective. But this is different, Victoria. You didn't just put yourself in the way of getting shot or even critically injured. You disobeying my order may have signed your death certificate." He ran his hand down his face. "I trust your skill and ability to defend yourself. You proved that at the Regal Institute and in the alley. But you have to understand that it is just as important to project the estimated outcome before you move forward. So before you disobey an order, you better have weighed the cost and are damn certain you've got a good chance of coming out alive."

He was right. I had flown out of the basement in pursuit and not given it a single thought to the probability that the man I was chasing down had just held Wren in that dank basement and was equipped do exactly what he had done to her, to me. I didn't even think to call on Ian and Carter, who were close enough to come to my aid.

"I'm sorry, Ian," I said softly. "You're right. It won't happen again." He wouldn't, or maybe couldn't, look at me. I suddenly felt very disconnected from him. Like we had entered the boss/employee zone.

"Good," he said flatly when he finally cast his gaze on me.

"Did *you* have something you wanted to say to *me*?" I prompted.

"I'm not sure I know what you're talking about," he said, averting his eyes again.

Before I could reprimand him fully, Carter jetted out of the room.

"Hey! Lovebirds! Save it for when we get the bad guy! Claudia's got something!" he barked.

I narrowed my eyes at Ian and met Claudia where we had left her. Strasser was also there.

"You're not going to believe this," she began. "That symbol is associated with a group out of St. Petersburg, Russia, and they are scary as hell. They call themselves Bratstvo Lenin."

"What does that mean?" I asked.

"It means Brotherhood of Lenin," Ian answered warily.

"As in Vladimir Lenin?" I clarified.

"Yes," he answered. I leaned on the table and cupped my hands over my mouth.

"With a love for the Motherland, I can't believe that all they're after is money," Carter remarked.

"You'd be right." Claudia pulled up an encrypted web site. "Their objective is rid the world of those who reject communist principles and start a new world under the, and I quote, 'only legitimate governance as established by the wise and powerful Lenin.' So, yeah, that's creepy. Also, they've been recruiting for decades." She turned her laptop around to reveal a surprisingly well-presented web site.

"They have a web site?" I questioned.

"Everyone who wants world domination starts with a web site. It's, like, in their manual," she replied. "And then they set it loose on the dark web for all the crazies to find."

"Who in the modern world would think this was a good idea?" I proposed. I turned and leaned against the table.

"Well," Claudia began. "Seems they've got a hefty monetary reward system for those who pledged their allegiance early and then dedicated their lives to recruiting for the cause."

"So who's running this monkey cult?" Carter quipped as he propped himself up and sat on the edge of the table.

"His name is Alexi Volkov," Claudia answered. "He's former KGB whose ideals got him kicked out for being too extreme."

My eyebrows nearly touched my hairline. "Too extreme for the KGB? Holy crap."

"Right? His manifesto on their web site reads like Lenin's Guide to Annihilating Civilians and Collapsing Democracy," she responded.

"Putin has made statements condemning Lenin's tactics, denouncing the brutal repressions by the Bolshevik government, and the Red Terror where Lenin killed thousands, some say half a million, who opposed him," Ian said. This was truly some scary stuff. "The rest of Volkov's cohorts all have varying degrees of connection to the Russian government. There's no pattern. Even Conway Harrison is a wild card. He came out of the UK banking scene 15 years ago. He's got no ties to the Communist Party. No connection to Russia at all."

"And by all accounts, they seem to have taken over the Regal Institute two years ago," Claudia said. "The board brought Harrison on as CFO, and then he pretty much staged a coup and fired everyone who had been there for legitimate reasons. Then he brought in the League of Deplorable Gentlemen and opened their Little Shop of Horrors."

"Nice." Carter said, fist bumping Claudia.

"Sounds like maybe he held the purse strings," I said. "Hold on a second. If their goal is to reboot Lenin's socialist revolution, then the only way they'll give the cure to anyone is if they pledge their loyalty to the Brotherhood, no matter how much the world's leaders pay. They have no intention of using the bacteria as just a means to make a cool billion and then go underground. They're going to use it to weed out the opposition."

Ian paced the room. "We know we're headed to St. Petersburg, but where do we go from there?" he mused aloud. He looked over Claudia's shoulder as she typed.

"Volkov's been putting his KGB skills to good use. He's a ghost. And as expected on the dark web, the IP address for the site jumps from continent to continent when you dig for it," she explained. "He's good."

"If the Brotherhood is behind this, they would have taken Wren to their base of operation," I offered. "They'd want first dibs on the cure before they made it available to members of their crazy club."

"Okay," Ian began. "Let's get to St. Petersburg and we'll go from there. I'll make contact with a Rogue team there and see if they've got any intel on Volkov."

Carter began gathering the files and documents spread out on the table, shoving them into a messenger bag. Claudia made contact with Command to arrange our transportation to Russia, while Ian called Thatcher about connecting with a team there. Me, I watched Strasser work frantically across the room. I wanted to think he was desperate to find the cure just for me, but the reality was that his anxiousness was 100% grounded in finding his daughter alive.

I picked up the paper I had drawn the symbol on and ran my finger over the crude sketch. Suddenly, it occurred to me where I had first seen the picture tattooed on Harrison's wrist. Nervousness tore through me, and Moreau's warning echoed in my mind. I was afraid I had discovered the *something that ran deeper than any of us could imagine*. The pieces were forming and I had to put them together. I called Ian to me.

"We're going to Dovstov," I told him quietly.

"How do you know this?"

"Because I remember where I first saw that symbol."

"That's wonderful, Victoria," he said. "Where?"

I swallowed hard. "On the paintings in Director Thatcher's office."

Chapter 18

Ian nodded at my information and began instructing Claudia. "We're going to a village outside St. Petersburg called Dovstov," he said.

"And how did we come up with this?" she asked, tilting her head to one side.

Ian looked at me before answering. "Victoria finally remembered seeing it in an old briefing I showed her during training."

"Great!" Claudia continued working at her laptop, presumably making changes to the order for our transportation.

"What are we doing with Strasser?" Carter asked. We all watched him work hurriedly across the room. He feverishly jotted notes, occasionally letting out an excited, "Yes!" when he remembered or discovered something. I wondered if he was making any progress or if he would need any more samples from me. "Someone has to stay with him." Three sets of eyes were on me. I almost behaved hastily and charged in on the offensive, but I took a breath and waited.

"I'll stay with him," Claudia said from behind them. "You need Vic there." Her response was confident and assured, and it didn't make me believe she was only supporting me going as some kind of girl-power move. She believed I would be able to serve the team best if I were on the ground in Dovstov with them.

"Well that settles that!" Carter spread a cheesy grin across his face and let out a laugh. He had revealed his admiration for Ian to me the day I was released from the hospital in Rome, so I knew what his true colors were. But regardless of how much he respected Ian, I think it would always give him a little chuckle when Ian was *informed* of what his decision would be.

Flight time for Rogue agents was also rest time, especially when you're on the red-eye. By the time we landed, it would have been almost forty-eight hours since Wren disappeared and 12 hours since I was infected with the bacteria. We were mentally and physically exhausted. We talked about the assignment as we boarded, and finalized a few things, but other than that, we all got into our own little world. Carter quickly shoved a pair of ear buds in, slouched in his seat, and closed his eyes. He may or may not have been listening to anything. I wouldn't put it past him to pretend he was so he could eavesdrop.

Ian's own little world still consisted of work. "I'll sleep when our mission is successful," he'd say. He pulled out the file Claudia had given him on the Brotherhood of Lenin. He had likely read everything in it four times before I finally spoke.

"Why didn't you tell them I saw the symbol in Thatcher's office?" I asked.

"Because there's nothing to tell," he answered, not looking up from the file.

"There's *something*, otherwise you would have told them," I countered.

He continued his focus on the papers in his hand. "Leave it alone, Victoria. There's nothing going on."

"Oh really?" I pulled the note I found in trash from my pocket and all but slapped it on the table. That got his attention.

He picked up the wrinkled paper. "What is this?"

"I found it in the trash in the basement," I told him. Ian examined it, setting his jaw tightly. "Can you explain it?"

"They're just messing with you," he said. "Trying to get in your head."

"Why *my* head? Why not yours or Carter's?" I countered. "They knew we would go there, and they knew I would be the one to find it. Add the fact that Thatcher has paintings in her office from someone connected to the Brotherhood of Lenin and—"

"Are you trying to accuse Thatcher of being some kind of double agent?" His question and tone were both sharp. "Do you know what that would mean?"

"She has acquired every painting in her office *personally*," I rebutted. "Thatcher knows *everything* about those pieces of art."

Ian let out a slow breath. "Victoria," he began. "Penny Thatcher is dedicated to INTERPOL and to the Rogue division. She is not a double agent. Now, I know you're probably a little skittish because of what happened with Damon, but—"

"This is not about Damon," I argued. "This is about you not being willing to connect the dots and believe that you could have been duped a second time." I wasn't wrong. There was some kind of connection between Thatcher and Volkov. Why couldn't Ian see that, or at least entertain the theory? If it were anyone else, he would have been all over it. "Look, we have a responsibility to explore this

connection. It doesn't matter that it's Thatcher. And …
maybe it *is* a little about Damon. If we had seen the signs or
made the connections early on…" I didn't want to say *then
maybe my brother would still be alive*. That may have been true.
But more than that, who knows how many people we could
be sparing from being trafficked.

Ian rested his elbows on the arms of his seat and
threaded his fingers together at his chest. He eyed me
cautiously, seeming to contemplate whether he should
follow the gut of a rookie agent on something that could be
so damaging.

"All right," he finally said. "But this is between us.
After what happened with Damon, an accusation like this
could bring down the whole Rogue division forever."

"I understand."

"So the first question is this: do you know the name of
the artist?"

"I don't. The signature was pretty illegible. It was the
symbol that stood out," I told him.

"Well," he began. "Let's see what the St. Petersburg
team has and we'll go from there. You should get some
rest. I need you alert when we arrive."

We landed on a private airstrip outside St. Petersburg
in the bright glow of sunrise, and were met by Travis
Hayes. He explained he was there leading a team
monitoring the Russian mob. I eyed Ian warily, knowing
how he felt about his days on assignment with the Italian
mob.

Guessing what I was thinking, Ian said, "The Russian
mob makes their Italian counterpart look like a Saturday
morning cartoon."

"Understood."

We drove through a city that looked like it could be
anywhere with shops at the street level of tall apartment or

office buildings, cars parked along the street, and traffic lights that weren't green nearly long enough. But then we crossed some mythical line and drove through a Russian storybook with green pastures, cottages, and horses with carts. The scene made me promise myself again that I would do my best to never become desensitized to the beauty of the world.

We entered another city-like area, although it was much smaller than the first. No tall buildings, but plenty of shops and other businesses. Travis pulled onto a narrow driveway in between two houses and parked in the back. The safe house looked like it was an extra room over a detached garage, but I knew better. Inside it would be outfitted with the latest technology and be staffed by some of the bravest and most skilled agents.

"Everyone," Travis announced as we entered the house. "This is Ian Hale, Victoria Asher, and Carter, uh…"

"Just Carter."

"Got it." Travis replied to Carter without flinching. Then he introduced his team. "This is Tarka Abdul, Bri Fisher, and Andy Clewell." We nodded in acknowledgement of one another. "They're looking for the Brotherhood of Lenin." Travis's team snickered.

"That's more of an urban legend," Tarka said. "There's been no sign of them in Russia for over 30 years, and even then they were a fledgling gang with ideals that every Russian leader *since* Lenin has rejected."

"Really?" Ian scoffed. He opened the file and laid pictures of the wrists of the man he killed in the alley as well as the one I had defeated. Both showed the symbol of the Brotherhood clearly. "Look familiar?"

Andy picked up one of the pictures and examined it. "What is this?" His New England accent was strong, making me assume he played the tourist part in every sting operation.

"It's the sign of the Brotherhood," Carter answered. "But you already knew that." He bore his eyes into Travis. If I knew anything about Carter, it was his disdain for team leaders who held out on sharing information.

"In addition to these two, at least one of a dozen men we detained at a lab in Belgium had the same marking," Ian continued.

"Have you seen this before?" I asked.

"Not in anything we've been monitoring," Tarka answered in a soft Middle Eastern accent. "Considering the connections the mob has to Putin, I'd say they're not involved. If the Brotherhood achieves their mission, Putin is out." Tarka looked at Bri and nodded toward a table behind them.

"But," she said. "It did show up in some outlying villages." Bri pulled a large envelope from a pile and slid a stack of pictures out. She flipped through them and laid them on the table. They were surveillance pictures of the crime family they had been following. In one, three men stood outside a run down building with a long fence behind them. From end to end, a dozen of the symbols had been spray-painted. In another, the symbol had been painted above the doors of a row of homes.

"And you didn't think to look into it further?" Carter suggested.

"Do you know how many revolutions are taking place in Russia at one time?" Tarka answered. "If we investigated every symbol of freedom that popped up, we'd never do anything else." The two men exchanged testosterone-filled looks before Ian stepped in.

"Travis, can we look through your surveillance? See what we can find?" Ian asked.

"Of course. Bri, get them whatever you have," he instructed. She returned to her desk and rummaged through files.

"Victoria." The simple sound of Ian saying my name needed no explanation. This is where I was supposed to shine. My heart quickened and I became anxious. This was not a drill. This was real. The lives of millions of people depended on it.

My life depended on it.

Bri handed me three large envelopes. "Start with these," she said. "When you're ready for more, I've got plenty."

"Thanks." I smiled appreciatively. "Hey ... uh ... can I ask where you're from?"

"Midwest," was all she said.

"Cool." Being so abruptly transplanted was, at times, difficult. There was something very comforting about meeting other Americans along this journey. "Are these in any particular order?" I nudged at the envelopes in my arms.

"The envelopes are divided by city or village."

"Any chance one of these is Dovstov?" I asked hopefully.

"Why Dovstov?" I couldn't tell if the expression on her face was that of curiosity or confusion.

"Just a lead we had," I told her.

She flipped through more envelopes, pulled one out, and handed it to me. It was much thinner than the others in my hand, and microscopic compared to the ones still left on her desk.

"If you can gather any real intel from a place like Dovstov, then you're a miracle worker," she said. "There's so little in that town that I've only seen one crime boss show his face there a handful of times over the course of a year."

"Well then, you should wish me luck." I laughed. Bri smiled and told me I could use the table next to her. So I took a seat and emptied the Dovstov envelope onto the surface before me.

Thirty. That's how many pictures there were. That was all I had to work with. I rubbed my hands together and got to work. The first few photos were curious. There were no people in them, and nothing of interest on or about the buildings. I set them aside to ask Bri about later. I didn't want to begin asking questions when the answers may reveal themselves in subsequent pictures.

I laid out the next ten pictures in what appeared to be succession, a series of photos showing the arrival, interaction, and departure of visitors to a small home. I identified the man in the expensive long, black coat and hat to be the subject of Travis's team, and the man in the cheap suit to be his henchman, the one whose hands got actual blood on them.

The henchman exited from the driver's door and opened the door for his boss. A man came from the home to greet them. He wore an apron and in one shot, had picked up the hem of it to wipe his hands.

"Hey Bri," I called. "Who is this?"

She looked over my shoulder at the picture I pointed to. "That's Boris Petrov, and that's Ivan Orlov. Nothing nefarious going on here. Boris is an art collector. He commissions a painting from Orlov every two or three months."

I nodded. "Okay. Um … and you guys have been in Orlov's place? Seen his work?"

"Yeah, it's not my cup of tea," she answered. "Tarka and I went in as collectors recommended to his work.

When we didn't find anything, we intercepted the shipment of one of his paintings to Petrov. We did everything to that painting. It went under a black light, had the corners of the canvas peeled ... even broke half the frame to see if it was hollowed out and hiding something. Nothing. The form letter we sent them both from the currier service apologizing for the damaged item was enough to make Petrov start to pick up his orders personally. We watched him for a while but still came up empty on anything illegal."

"Thanks." I sighed. I squished my face with my hands and then ran my fingers through my hair. I was about to move on to the next pictures in the stack when I noticed something in the third picture of the sequence: Petrov was not alone in the back seat of that car. When Petrov stepped out and stood next to the car, I could see the crossed legs of a woman. And then my heart leaped into my throat.

I'd recognize that stilettoed foot anywhere.

Chapter 19

I stood with the picture in my hand, ready to take what I believed was evidence against Thatcher to Ian. I found him with Travis on the other side of the house discussing something unrelated to our assignment. I watched them for a moment, enjoying how admired and respected Ian was by others. I counted to four, letting myself have only those seconds to be a proud girlfriend. When it was over, my agent hat was back on and I was a woman on a mission.

"Ian," I called to him. I held the picture up, indicating I had found something. He excused himself from Travis and met me where I stood, a good six feet from them.

"What did you find?" he asked, taking the picture from me.

"The big guy is some mob boss named Boris Petrov. The messy one? That's Ivan Orlov, our painter," I told him.

"Anything else?"

"Yeah. Look inside the car." I watched as Ian looked closer. When he saw it, he set his exasperated eyes on me. "You're not honestly telling me that you think this is Thatcher. There's no way you can prove it's her."

"There's no way you can prove it's not." I folded my arms and pressed my lips together.

Ian drew in a breath that I'm sure was meant to keep him from yelling at me. "Let's stay focused here. Whether Thatcher knew what was going on when she acquired those paintings is secondary right now. Our objective is to find Wren and stop Natalia and Harrison's associates from releasing the virus. Can we agree on that?"

I swallowed my pride. "Yes."

"Good. Now, we need to get into this studio." Ian turned around. "Travis?"

Ian's conversation with Travis led us back to Bri and Tarka. They explained to him everything Bri had already told me about Petrov and Orlov. They were unclear what we could find that they had not.

"You were looking for connections to Petrov and other mob leaders. We're looking for one small symbol that you would have thought nothing of, had you seen it," I said. Bri and Tarka agreed. "Now, can you get us in? I have a sudden thirst for a one-of-a-kind piece of art."

Tarka made a call to Orlov and told him he had some friends in town that he thought would be interested in his work. He arranged for us to visit the studio that afternoon. I didn't want there to be too much time between Tarka's call and our visit so he didn't have time to hide anything that might associate him with the Brotherhood, but to rush the timing would have put him on edge.

We arrived at Orlov's home/studio at one o'clock, having changed our clothes and looking much more like a couple prepared to spare no expense for an original piece of artwork.

Orlov answered almost immediately after Ian knocked.

"Zdravstvuyte. Orlov?" Ian said in perfect Russian.

"Da. Smith?" He replied.

Ian nodded then asked, "Ty govorish' po-angliyski?"

Orlov smiled. "Yes. But you may have to excuse me if my English is a little broken." We all smiled and laughed lightly as Orlov welcomed us into his home and studio.

"Thank you, Mr. Orlov," I said in a British accent. Ian shot me a look.

"Please. You must call me Ivan," he insisted.

I smiled pleasantly. "Thank you, *Ivan.*" He was a pleasant man, around forty, with light brown hair and hazel eyes. He didn't look old enough to have any long-standing allegiance to the Brotherhood.

Ivan led us through his living room to a door in the back of the house. The living space was small and the furnishings were nothing to speak of. There was no artwork displayed. I didn't expect him to necessarily display his own work, but there was literally nothing on any wall. That didn't automatically mean something bad. I just thought it odd.

We passed through a door and were ushered into a glorious art studio. Canvases and frames, canisters filled with brushes, and tables with bottles of paint illustrated this almost magical space. Ivan's paintings lined the perimeter of the studio, while a work in progress sat on the large easel at the end of the room.

"Oh my," I said. "It's breathtaking."

"Which piece to like?" Ivan asked.

I smiled at him. "All of them!"

He actually blushed a little and then invited us to meet him at his easel. I again saw the lines and shapes that drew Thatcher to his work. This piece wasn't done yet, so he hadn't yet signed it. But I looked at the paintings that lined the perimeter of the room. Some signatures had the Brotherhood of Lenin symbol while others didn't. I didn't understand.

"Looks like you've got a lot of clients waiting for their artwork." I motioned to the canvases along the wall and smiled. Something was different about the paintings with the Brotherhood symbol. In certain areas, the paint was thicker, almost protruding off the canvas. I reached out to touch one of the bubbles.

"PLEASE!" he shouted. "Don't touch those." I smiled sheepishly and stepped back to Ian's side. "Those are for a gallery showing tomorrow at Erarta, the Museum of Contemporary Art. Once a month they host a gallery for local Russian artists." He smiled proudly. "I've been waiting six months for this showing."

"That's wonderful. You must be very excited." Ian looked at me and smiled.

"Yes. It is very exciting. I can show which ones are available from this collection. There are several already at the gallery, though," Ivan said.

I read Ian's mind and knew we were thinking the same thing. "Perhaps, since we're not looking to commission a piece, it would be better for us to attend the gallery exhibit. The timing seems to be perfect." I coated my voice with hope.

"That would be very good," Ivan said. "You can get in a bidding war for your favorite piece!" he laughed.

"Shall we contact the museum directly for tickets?" I asked.

"Here," Ivan said. He walked to a desk, opened a drawer, and pulled out a small stack of tickets. "Please, come as my guests, five o'clock, and bring Tarka and Bri. I would be honored." He handed Ian four tickets.

"That's very kind of you. We will definitely be there." The two men shook hands as Ivan gave Ian the tickets. Ivan shook my hand and then escorted us to the door.

As we pulled away from the curb, I watched Ivan in the side mirror. He waved once and then returned into his home. There was nothing off about him, but the fact that only some of his paintings had the symbol of the Brotherhood had me worried.

"The symbol wasn't on all the paintings. Obviously some of them are for the Brotherhood and others are not. The question is, why would they be differentiated that way?" Ian posed. "What is it about those pieces that separates them from the others?"

"There was something different about the Brotherhood paintings," I said. "A different technique than I saw on Thatcher's paintings or on the others there in the studio. There were three to four places on those painting that were thick with paint. It was weird, and didn't feel like just an artistic choice. I'm going to need to get a closer look."

"You'll get your chance tomorrow," Ian said. I sighed and shook my head. "What is it?"

"I feel bad for him," I said. "Whatever his involvement with the Brotherhood, I don't think it's by choice."

"Everyone has a choice."

Chapter 20

I took the simple, black sheath dress Bri offered and slipped it on. It fit a little too much like a glove, and I wasn't sure how I was supposed to carry my gun. I picked up the black sequined clutch purse in one hand and my gun in the other. Realizing the clutch was my only option, I slid my gun inside and let out a small laugh. *Lipstick. Compact. Gun. What else would I carry?*

Stepping out of the bedroom, I found that Adam had arrived. He was standing around a table with the rest of the teams being debriefed on the plan.

"Damn, girl!" Carter exclaimed.

Ian shot him a look. "That's enough, Carter."

"I'm just saying, your woman is smokin' hot!"

I finished rolling my eyes just as Ian met me where I stood. He surprised me by kissing my cheek softly and then whispering in my ear. "He's right. You look ravishing." I blushed and smiled and let the butterflies take up residence in the pit of my stomach for just a moment. When Ian pulled away, he gave a quick wink and then invited me to join them.

"You guys clean up pretty well yourselves," I said. The men all looked like James Bond in their tuxes, and Bri's red, sleeveless slip dress was gorgeous.

"Andy and Adam are going in as contract security. They'll be able to monitor the entire event with a more probing eye and not have it questioned. Travis will monitor the security cameras and gather intel on any guests showing particular interest in the Brotherhood paintings," Ian said. "Carter will fly solo, and Victoria and I will attend with Tarka and Bri as their guests. Hopefully this will disarm Orlov and get us even closer to him."

"Are you sure you want to join in on this?" I asked Travis of his team's involvement.

"Petrov was with your painter. We may not have seen a connection before, but there may be something there," he said. "And we're all about saving the world so ... anything we can do help." Travis gave me a small smile and I reciprocated gratefully. This thing was huge, and we were going to need all the help we could get.

Andy and Adam wore earpieces with coiled wires that hung behind their ears, which were more in line with what security personnel would wear. The rest of us nestled flesh colored, voice activated pieces into our ears and exited the safe house.

Tarka, Ian, Bri, and I climbed into a black sedan and made our way into St. Petersburg. I crossed my legs and glanced at my shoes. Furrowing my brow, I turned to Bri next to me in the back seat and asked, "You got any tips for running in these things? You know ... just in case."

"Yeah," she said. "Take them off." We smiled and chuckled at the absurdity.

Before I knew it, we were pulling up outside of Erarta. It was a huge and majestic looking structure, as so many of the buildings in St. Petersburg were. Stately columns greeted us at the front entry on the first floor, and larger ones extended from the second to the top. Windows lined in perfect rows covered the entire front of the building. But there was something so streamlined and modern about the building as well. Were it not for the columns, I would assume it was an apartment building.

We checked in and handed a middle-aged woman our tickets. We entered the museum, and my "apartment building" impression flew out the window. It was sleek and modern and unique. Each section was designed for something specific, whether it was paintings or sculptures or interactive pieces. I was impressed.

With my arm hooked through Ian's, we strolled through the gallery until we found the section set apart for just Ivan Orlov's work, picking up flutes of champagne from a server along the way. Soft Russian chatter from patrons filled the air. I was grateful to have Ian and the others to translate, but I determined that I could not rely on always having someone around me who spoke the language. I would have to commit myself to learning new languages if I wanted to maintain my career as a Rogue agent.

"I thought there'd be more vodka here," Carter said in our ears.

"Of course you did." I raised my glass at him. "Now, do your job and go flirt with someone."

From across the room, Carter tipped his imaginary hat to me and began putting the moves on a gorgeous blonde standing next to him.

The white walls of the gallery made Orlov's paintings pop. His work was filled with bright colors and abstract shapes. They reminded me of Jackson Pollock, but Orlov's lines felt more deliberate and weren't nearly as busy as Pollock's. I counted twenty-five paintings in total. I would need to examine each one to determine how many had the symbol of the Brotherhood of Lenin. Would each of those have the same bulging pockets as the one I saw in the studio?

Orlov saw us and made a beeline in our direction.

"Welcome," he said. "I am so happy you were able to make it. Tarka … Bri." He shook Tarka's hand and kissed Bri on the cheek. "Perhaps you'll find a piece here that will speak to your heart."

"I do hope so!" Bri said. "I'm sorry I'm so fickle." We all laughed.

"No, no! Do not be sorry. Art must speak to your soul," Orlov said reassuringly. I'd never seen such a collection of fake smiles exchanged between people.

Someone called to Orlov and he excused himself from us.

"I have eyes on Petrov." Andy's voice rang in our ears. "He's on the north end of the gallery."

Ian and I casually made our way toward Petrov. I noted four pieces with the Brotherhood symbol on that side of the gallery, and ten without. When we were close enough to Petrov, I "accidentally" bumped into him, causing his champagne to slosh in his glass and splash onto his jacket.

"Oh my goodness!" I declared. "I am so very sorry!" I took my napkin and attempted to wipe the spot where his drink had landed.

"No, no," Petrov said in his thick, Russian accent. "It is fine. Only an accident."

"You're too kind," I said. I extended my hand. "My name is Victoria Smith and this is my husband, Ian."

Boris took my hand in his. "Boris Petrov. It is my pleasure." The cuff of his sleeve slid up his wrist slightly, allowing me to look for a tattoo that would match

Harrison's. His other hand reached up, brushing away the drops of champagne that had landed on his lapel. Nothing. At least we were able to rule out one person.

While Boris shook Ian's hand, I noticed the lovely woman standing next to him. She was tall and thin with all the features of a European model. I admired her dress and then ... her shoes.

"Are you coveting her shoes, darling?" Ian asked with a smile. "My wife adores a stylish stiletto, don't you, dear?"

I was both gutted and relieved to be wrong about the woman in the car with Petrov. But I still didn't have any explanation as to why Thatcher had Orlov's paintings with the Brotherhood symbol. The quest for that answer would have to stay on the back burner for now.

"Oh, yes." I mirrored his expression. The girl smiled back, kissed Boris on the cheek and then walked away.

"She's a woman of few words," he explained.

"Are you a fan of Ivan's or just a lover of art?" Ian asked.

"I am partial to Ivan's work," Boris answered. "We are from the same village. Collecting his paintings is like having pieces of home with me now that I live here in St. Petersburg."

There was a spark in Boris' eyes when he spoke of the connection with his home village. He loved his country and, while a Russian mobster, wouldn't wish the people of his youth to be annihilated.

"That's so lovely," I said.

"Now, if you'll excuse me. It was very nice to meet you." Boris nodded and gave us a pleasant smile before stepping away.

"All right, Victoria," Travis said in my ear. "Time to identify the Brotherhood paintings and get a glimpse of those showing interest in them."

I looked at Ian and smiled adoringly. "Let's get this show on the road."

Piece by piece I toured the gallery with Ian, stopping to admire only the paintings with the Brotherhood symbol. Travis ran the faces of anyone who stopped to examine those paintings through facial recognition. Travis would pull up their information and give us their name. Tarka and Bri would confirm if they were subjects they had been tracking, which at this point showed no connection to the Brotherhood of Lenin. But most of them weren't suspected of anything.

"Roman Gorev and Sergei Katin," Travis said.

"Doesn't ring a bell," Bri said, as if she were talking to Tarka.

My gut flipped at the mention of those names. When I turned and saw the two men standing in front of the painting to my right, I knew exactly how I knew them.

"I know those names," I said. "They were part of the Regal Institute. I saw their pictures on the wall there. They must have already been here when we raided the lab."

Gorev and Katin moved away from the painting and out of Orlov's gallery space. Ian made eye contact with Carter, who had been flirting with another supermodel, and gave him silent instructions to follow the two men. Adam followed close behind.

"I need to get close enough to one of his Brotherhood paintings to figure out what's so special about these specific paintings," I said. "It can't just be that they've got the symbol of the Brotherhood in the signature."

"Tarka … Bri," Ian said just loud enough for them to hear through their earpieces. They sauntered over to us, handing Ian a flute of champagne.

"Be careful, dear, you don't want to end up tipsy." I smirked.

"Oh, darling, if anyone here can hold their alcohol, it's me."

"You've clearly never been drinking with Carter."

He echoed my expression and leaned in like he was going to kiss my cheek. "Be quick."

The three of them covered me as I stepped closer to the painting in front of us that included the symbol of the Brotherhood of Lenin in Orlov's signature. Tarka, Bri, and Ian turned their backs to me and created as much of a barrier as possible. I examined all four of the protruding bubbles of paint from the canvas. Then, after quickly looking over my shoulder, I reached my hand up and gently pushed on the small bubble of paint. The tension reminded me of a mostly-filled water balloon. It was firm to the touch, but not solid.

I furrowed my brow. Why the change in his design? Everything about these paintings was similar to the others except for the bubble. Only the canvases with the symbol included this change.

Then it hit me.

"Ian" I whispered as I turned around. He stepped intimately closer to me. "It's the antidote."

"What?" he questioned.

"The antidote," I reiterated. "This must be how they're distributing the cure to the upper level leadership."

"They've only just gotten their hands on Wren," he argued. "There's no way they'd have time to get it to Orlov to put in the paintings."

"Strasser said he created the cure and then destroyed everything that was left along with the research. Orlov could have the initial doses. They need Wren for the rest," I said.

Ian looked at the painting and then looked at me. He whispered, "How many of the Brotherhood paintings did you see in the studio?"

I thought back to the previous day and closed my eyes. I could see the studio and the paintings along the perimeter of the room. "Seven, maybe eight."

"With four pockets in each, that's a max of twenty-four doses," Bri said.

"We have to find out how they plan on distributing the cure to the rest of their followers," Tarka declared.

"I know exactly how. Gorev and Katin."

Chapter 21

Ian and I looked at each other and immediately moved in the direction Gorev and Katin were headed. Carter and Adam would have hopefully already caught up with them. Now that I was certain about Orlov using the paintings to smuggle the cure to the Brotherhood, their interrogation techniques were sure to lead us to Wren and their supply of the antidote. I would administer a dose to myself and destroy the rest. Without it, their plan would be futile.

We got to the back of the building and I stopped. My head began to throb behind my eyes. I closed them and inhaled deeply.

"Are you okay?" Ian placed his hand on my back as he asked.

"Yeah, I'm fine." I lied. "Just considering where we go from here." Did we enter a restricted area on that floor, or should we make our way up?

"Carter," Ian said.

"Take the stairs down," he said.

We eased down the linoleum stairs, my heels lightly clacking on each step. The basement of the building was a far cry from the one in Brussels. It was clean and sterile, and climate controlled for priceless works of art stored in crates and boxes around every room we came to. Before we reached the fourth room, Carter and Adam were in our ears, but not speaking to us.

"Down on the ground!" Adam yelled. Gunfire echoed off the walls. We followed the sound and found Adam and Carter ambushed by four men, while Gorev and Katin frantically put vials of the cure in a cooler in a replica of Strasser's lab at the Regal Institute.

I pulled my gun and told them to stop. "Make another move, and I swear to God I'll treat each one of those tubes like it's target practice." They stopped and lifted their hands shoulder-height in the air. Carter, Ian, and Adam continued their scuffle, snapping one man's neck and leaving him in a pile on the floor. Another of them came barreling toward me. I used his force in motion against him and sent him headlong into the concrete wall, knocking him out and sending me stumbling to the floor. Gorev and Katin took their opportunity and ran from the room. The two goons left escaped with them.

"You have to stop them! They took vials of the cure with them," I shouted. Carter and Adam sprinted for the door. "Go!" I barked at Ian. "I'm going to look for Wren."

Ian nodded confidently and bolted after Carter and Adam in pursuit of the scientists and their thugs.

After surveying the lab, I was convinced Wren was somewhere in that building. There was no way they were going to keep her far from where they could take her blood and then separate the antidote from it. And by the looks of this set up, they could take a fair amount to work with at once. They could take as much blood as possible and process it while her body made more. If there was one thing I remembered from high school biology, it was that it took twenty-four hours for the human body to replace lost blood. In the meantime, she would be weak and light headed. Even if they didn't have her strapped to a table, she'd be too frail to escape on her own.

I dusted myself off, readied my gun, and continued through the basement. I had taken four steps when I decided to preemptively take Bri's advice and kick off my shoes. I didn't know what was waiting for me, and I needed to be prepared.

The basement consisted of room after room that extended the length of the museum itself. It was massive, and I was losing hope. Then a man appeared from another room. He was dressed in a tux just like the goons who attacked my guys. He had obviously been sent down to make sure everything was okay after the other henchmen didn't report back. He saw me and reached for his gun. Without hesitation I pulled my trigger and shot him in the chest. Hearing the commotion, a woman exited the same room. She was dressed in scrubs, like a nurse … and my attackers in Brussels. Her wide eyes told me she was shocked and scared.

"Let me see your hands," I ordered. At the very least she understood English, because she held her hands up in surrender. "Hold out your arms in front of you with your palms up." Again she did as she was told. Keeping my gun trained on her, I examined her wrists. No signed of the Brotherhood of Lenin. But that didn't mean she wasn't loyal to their cause. I wondered if this was how she was paying for her dosage of the cure. "Do you speak English?" I continued. She nodded. "Is there anyone else in that room I should be worried about? And before you lie to me, consider what I did to your friend here."

"No. No one," she said. Her Russian accent wasn't as strong as Boris' had been, but it was quite prominent.

I waved my gun toward the room. "Inside."

I stepped over the thug I had shot and followed her into the room. I couldn't believe what I was seeing. It was as if I had stepped into a high tech hospital room. Beeping monitors and computer screens on both sides, and a hospital bed in the center where Wren Strasser lay. A bag of fluid was connected to one of her arms while the other had a catheter set up and ready to be used to draw blood at a moment's notice.

I found some tubing in a drawer and tied the nurse's hands behind her back and her ankles to a chair. "Don't do anything that's going to force me to shoot you."

Then, I put my gun down on the bed and attended to Wren.

She was pale and looked weak. Her eyes were dark, like death; her lips white and flaky from being dehydrated. And her skin felt like ice. But, she was breathing and semiconscious, her eyes just slits, which was all that mattered.

I didn't know what I should have expected when I found her, but her condition shook me to the core. We had to get her out of there and to a legitimate hospital.

"Ian," I said. I waited for him to respond in my ear. When he didn't, I realized that I hadn't heard them at all since they left me in the lab down the hall. I reached up and discovered that my earpiece was missing. It was must have fallen out when I was knocked to the ground. *Shit.*

"Vic..." Wren's voice rasped.

"Okay ... it's okay, Wren," I said to her.

"Char..."

"I know," I said softly. "I'm so sorry. But Ian is going to be back any minute, and we're going to get you out of here. And then we'll take you to see your dad, and everything will be okay."

I took her icy hand in mine and squeezed it gently. She returned the gesture, even though infinitesimally.

The rapid whizzing and darting sound of a bullet being fired from a gun with a silencer on it startled me. But I wasn't nearly as startled as the poor nurse who had just taken a bullet to the head.

I reached for my gun.

"Don't." A familiar female voice snapped. In walked Natalia, looking a little less put together than the first time I had seen her. Of course, that was my doing since I was the one who had tackled her and created the welt on the side of her face.

"How the hell are you here?" I questioned.

"Please. You think that plant on your man Carter's team was our only inside man?" she laughed. "Half that police department in Brussels is on our payroll. How do you think we found our test subjects? Poor runaways. Disappearing. Never to be found again." She plastered a sinister grin across her face. "They also made sure I was halfway to Russia with my daughter when you were just putting it together about the apartment."

"You really are a smug bitch, aren't you?"

"No. I'm just British."

"So what's your plan, psycho? You're going to smuggle the antidote to the Brotherhood of Lenin bigwigs and then, what? Make the rest of their followers *pay* for the cure?" I questioned.

"Everything has its price."

"You really believe in what the Brotherhood stands for?"

"Oh, God, no." She waved her non-gun-toting hand dismissively. "I'm a scientist. I think this concept of annihilating a people is fascinating. And the brilliance of the accelerated bacteria—Jeremy is a genius!"

I shook my head in disgust. "So it's all about science and not the shit ton of money they're paying you."

She smiled devilishly. "Well, there's also that."

Righteous anger boiled inside me. For the Brotherhood, it was about creating a pure race under Lenin's principles and regime guidelines. For her, it was partly about science, but mostly about money. And she was sacrificing her own daughter's life for it all.

"Now," she continued. "Untie the poor girl and bind your own wrists with the same skill you did hers."

I turned toward the dead nurse and evaluated my surroundings. My gun still lay on the bed by Wren's legs, not that it mattered. Natalia would fire off a silent round at me before I could get a grip on my weapon. I needed to get her gun out of her hand. Then it would be a fair fight. But how?

As I knelt behind the chair and started to untie the nurse, I spotted a tray. It was the stainless steel kind normally reserved for medical tools like scalpels and that clampy thing nurses gripped gauze with to blot blood and fluid. This tray, however, was empty. I took a breath and inhaled all the bravery I could.

In one fluid motion I stood, grabbed the tray, and flung it at Natalia like a Frisbee. In true Victoria Asher form, I aimed for her head. I nailed her right across the forehead with a ding. While she was stunned, I lunged for her and knocked the gun from her hand. We tumbled to the floor. I expected to dominate her as I did outside the Regal Institute, but I had really pissed her off this time, and she was not having it. She gripped my hair in her fist and twisted our bodies, slamming my head against the nearby cabinets. Then she scurried across the floor as she went for her gun. I grabbed her leg and slid her backward. It was easy to do on the slick linoleum floors. Her body lay in front of me in perfect position for my elbow to make contact with her ribs. I drove my arm down and cracked her side as hard as I could. Her body buckled and she turned to the side.

Thinking she was going to nurse her wound, I stood and took a step toward her gun. Instead, she spun her body around and swept her legs under mine, bringing me plunging down onto my back. The cracking of my skull making contact with the floor echoed eerily in my ears and exacerbated the pain I was already trying to ignore. When I stopped seeing stars, I saw Natalia over me ... pointing her gun at my head.

"Stand up!" she yelled. Her menacing Lady Tramaine tone had been replaced by a psychotic, and very pissed off, Cruella De Vil.

I stood and tried to catch my breath, willing the agonizing beat in my head to end. I looked over at Wren; although weak, she was still able to show emotion. Tears streamed from the corners of her eyes to her ears as she lay there. I couldn't imagine her pain. Not from being poked and prodded like a lab rat, but from knowing it was her own flesh and blood causing it with no remorse.

"You silly little girl," Natalia continued. "The clock is ticking and time is running out for you."

"You left the note."

"It added a little something special to your experience, don't you think?" she teased. I lurched forward, ready for another battle. She steadied her gun at me. "Ah, ah, ah. I'd much rather know you died a painful death as the bacteria has its way with you, but if I have to shoot you, I will."

Suddenly, a wave a relief came over me. The fear she had thrust upon me dissipated and a smile made its way across my face.

"Coming to terms with your fate, dear?" she asked.

"No. Just enjoying this last moment of watching you believe you've won," I said. "You should never assume that your target is alone." A gun cocked behind Natalia and the barrel pressed into her head as I smiled at Ian. The shock of defeat that washed over Natalia's face was everything I needed to make the aches in my body subside for just a moment.

Ian pulled Natalia's arm behind her back and took her gun. Carter and Adam charged into the room, followed by paramedics. In a flash, they had transferred Wren to a smaller bed and rolled her out. Adam went with her to make sure she was safe. Ian kept his hand firmly on Natalia's cuffed wrists as we walked back to the main gallery floor, where he asked Travis to keep an eye on her.

The gallery was swarming with INTEROPL agents and Russian police. In the time since they had left me in the basement, Ian and Travis's teams had apprehended Roman Gorev and Sergei Katin, along with fifteen other high-ranking members of the Brotherhood of Lenin. Orlov was in custody but yelling about having only helped them in order to save his own family, which was quite possibly true.

No one had divulged where the bacteria was being kept, but since the cure hadn't been fully distributed to the Brotherhood's leaders, it was safe to say assume that we weren't in danger of it having been released yet. And, with the cure securely in our hands, their plan of annihilating everyone but those who swore allegiance to the Brotherhood was futile.

"A team from the World Health Organization just arrived to manage the antidote here and another is at the hospital to help with Wren. I'm going to follow Natalia all the way through with INTERPOL," Ian told me. "I want to make sure there's no interception with her delivery to a prison cell this time."

"I wouldn't worry too much about that," I replied. "Once the Russian authorities find out she was orchestrating an overthrow of their beloved government, I'm sure they won't let her out of their sight." My eyelids grew heavy and my breathing was becoming shallow.

"Are you sure you're okay?" he asked. He pressed the back of his hand to my forehead. "You feel warm and your face is flushed."

"Yeah. She just really kicked my ass back there." I chuckled.

"Just ... go see the medic before..." He brushed my cheek with the back of his hand. I took his hand in mine and smiled.

"I'm fine, Ian. Really. There's plenty of time."

"If you say so. I'm not sure how long this is going to take, so I'll see you back in London." Ian kissed me on the cheek and met Travis where he stood with Natalia. I eyed her triumphantly and watched as Ian pushed her along and out the front door.

I lowered my chin to my chest and struggled to take a breath to keep myself from vomiting.

"All right, liar," Carter said. "Let's go." He took my hand and led me back to the basement stairs. He had just opened the door to the stairwell when I couldn't hold myself up any longer.

"Carter," I breathed out as my knees buckled. He caught me before my body made contact with the floor, and then scooped me up and rushed me down the stairs.

"No way, girl. You are *not* going anywhere," he declared.

I was in and out of full consciousness, trying to calculate how many hours had really passed since I was infected. At most it had been 46 hours. Or was it?

"She needs a dose of that *now!*" Carter barked as we entered the lab. He set me down in a chair and shouted again when he saw they were looking at him like deer caught in headlights. "I said she needs that antidote now!"

"We haven't confirmed or stabilized—" one of the technicians said.

"I don't give a shit what you think you need to do! That's the cure, and she needs it. Now, you either give it to her, or I will pry it from your cold, dead fingers and do it myself!"

Through tired eyes, I watched them insert a syringe into the small bottle and fill the tube with the clear liquid. Within seconds, the needle pierced my skin and the sting of the antidote rushed in.

"You should have one too," I said to Carter. "All of you should. Just to be safe." I may have crossed the threshold into being contagious, and it was better to be safe than sorry.

Carter took his shot like a champ and knelt down next to me. "If you could stop almost dying, that'd be great." He let out a breathy laugh and pushed the hair out of my face. His fingers trailed my cheek and then down my arm to my hand. He threaded his fingers in mine and I leaned my head onto his shoulder. "Oh, newbie. What am I going to do with you?"

Chapter 22

The kettle whistled loudly, beckoning me from beneath the plush blanket I had found refuge under. My London flat had never felt so homey. I wondered if it would always be this way: go out on assignment, face great peril, come home, cozy up under a blanket. It seemed like a strange progression, but if in the end I landed on my couch, binge-watching Netflix with a cup of Earl Grey tea in my hand, then I could live with that.

My laptop dinged with a notification, and the bar telling me that I had a new email slid in from the top right corner. It was from Claudia, and the subject line read, "Being a Badass & Other Things You Should Know." I let out a breathy laugh and opened the message. The short body of the email intentionally read like a parody of a cheesy greeting card. Below that, however, was an update on Damon. My heart quickened and I began reading like a mad woman.

Slow down, Vic. You're going to miss something.

I stopped, closed my eyes, and just breathed. Then, I read.

The long and short of it was that Claudia had tracked Damon to Greece, and that in the weeks leading up to him showing his face, there had been an increase of missing persons reports, just as there had been in Italy. She cautioned me to be patient and to keep her little spying efforts under wraps.

I scrolled down and clicked on the first image she sent. It was Damon, dressed in a white suit and fedora, casually having drinks with two men. Being that they were in Damon's company, I could only assume they were as devious as he was. The second picture was of him speaking with a girl around my age. She was beautiful, with sun-kissed skin and long, golden hair. She had no idea the type of man she was face to face with. Surely this was an encounter that was about to lead to destroying her life.

A knock came at the door, startling me out of my trance of fury. I clicked out of the email and then closed my laptop. When I opened the door, Ian was standing there with a huge bouquet of tulips.

I smiled. "Oh, Ian! They're beautiful!"

"I should be delivering these to you in a hospital," he chastised right before he kissed me gently.

"Carter got me back to London and made me stay overnight at the hospital for observation," I told him. "He even stayed with me all night so I wouldn't pull a Houdini."

"Oh he did, did he?" Ian raised a suspicious eyebrow.

"Please. It's Carter." I shot Ian a look to remind him of my love-hate relationship with Carter. "Anyway ... by yesterday morning all my blood tests came back normal and I was free to go. I've been cozied up under my blanket binge-watching *Friends* and drinking tea ever since."

"I'm sorry I wasn't here to take care of you," he said with a disappointed sigh. We sat close together on the couch, finding our place as civilians in love and not secret agents clumsily navigating through love and danger.

"It's okay. That's the nature of the job," I said. "So I'm assuming everything got squared away and Natalia won't ever see the light of day."

"Pretty much," Ian replied. "And Jeremy and Wren Strasser are safe in a flat in Oxford. She'll return to school when she's ready, and Jeremy is taking some time off. I think they both need it."

"So ... I guess I owe you and apology for accusing Thatcher," I said sheepishly.

"Not at all."

I knit my brows together. "What?"

"Based on the information you had, you made a call. It wasn't bad information either, Victoria," he said. "But for where we were, following a lead to point the finger at Thatcher wasn't going to help us."

"Yeah, but I was wrong," I admitted.

"We don't know that."

"Okay. Now you're worrying me."

"I was in Thatcher's office this morning and saw the symbol on three of her paintings," he told me. "I told her we made the connection to the Brotherhood of Lenin based on something Natalia let slip, which led us to Russia. And that collaborating with Travis's team gave us the evidence we needed to get us to the gallery."

"You lied to her?" That was very unlike Ian. He respected Thatcher and the position she held with INTERPOL and the Rogue division.

"I altered the facts," he answered hesitantly.

"Why would you do that?"

He thought for a moment before he answered. "Thatcher purchased those paintings long before Strasser developed the bacteria and its cure. To say she was involved in that plot is a stretch, but ... knowing that Orlov added the symbol for Brotherhood followers gives me pause. There are questions to be answered. Did she purchase those paintings because she carries some allegiance to the Brotherhood? Or were they prepared for someone else and Thatcher came in and offered him more than he was going to get?"

"So what do we do?" I asked nervously.

"Now I'm going to do what I specifically told you not to do: I'm going to do a little digging."

I gave him a crooked smile. "Why, Ian Hale! You sneaky, sneaky man!" I laughed and then took his hand in mine. "Actually … I know that's not easy for you."

"I feel confident it's going to be the latter of the options," he said. "Thatcher is a woman who gets what she wants."

I didn't know what to say. My gut was still churning with suspicion. I didn't want to feel that way. Thatcher had believed in me and my ability to be a good Rogue agent when I was convinced my greatest skill was memorizing the entire menu for The Clock Diner. She gave me the opportunity to have a life after I had lost everything. So I didn't say anything at all.

"On to more important things," Ian said with a refreshing smile. "How are you feeling?"

"I'm good, actually," I told him. "I've been resting and getting plenty of fluids … not that the hospital didn't flood my system with plenty while I was there." I rolled my eyes recalling the six bags they gave me in 14 hours. "My body is a little drained, but overall I'm great."

"I'm so pleased," he said sweetly.

"So … now that we're back from this assignment, what do we do? Do I continue training? Do we go into Command and just wait for someone to do something nefarious somewhere in the world? How does this work?"

"We'll go back into the office when I'm convinced you're well enough to do some more training," he answered. "There's usually very little time in between assignments, but we'll just wait to hear from Thatcher."

I turned toward Ian and pushed the blanket to the side. "However will we pass the time?"

"I'm quite sure I can figure something out, Miss Asher," Ian said with a sexy smile. "I'd hate for you to be bored."

"Yes, boredom is the worst." I twisted my body and threw a leg over Ian, straddling his lap. I took his face in my hands, while he took my whole body in his, and kissed him passionately. "If this is how the waiting period is going to go, I'll never be bored."

"Thumb war?" he suggested.

"Really? Okay," I said suspiciously. "But I'm going to need a minute to think of some secret to divulge."

"We'll see." Ian brought his hand from behind my back and we hooked our fingers together. Within seconds, I had won.

"You gave me that win," I laughed.

"Maybe." A soft and playful smile appeared on Ian's face. "I love you."

"That's not a secret."

"The secret is that I've known I loved you since that day in bakery."

I couldn't have stopped smiling if I tried.

In that moment, every worry and concern I had for Ian's and my ability to navigate our relationship and our jobs as Rogue agents disappeared. We had successfully completed a mission that had taken us from London to Brussels to St. Petersburg. I had nearly died … again. And I had managed to go undercover and save a man and his daughter.

I had been unsure about this life going into it. But now, being there with Ian on the other side of more danger than I knew existed, I knew everything was going to be okay. Ian and I were a team and, together, we were going to save the world, one mission at a time.

About the Author

AnnaLisa is the youngest of four children and the only daughter, born and raised in Fort Lauderdale, Florida. After graduating high school, she moved to Charlotte, NC with her parents. This turned out to be a blessing since it was just a few short years later that she met her husband in the Film Actor's Studio of Charlotte. As she studied acting at the Studio, AnnaLisa was in several films and made-for-TV movies, as well as performed in local theater in both dramatic and musical roles.

AnnaLisa's publicist is Rick Miles of Red Coat PR, and she is represented by Italia Gandolfo of GH Literary. AnnaLisa has been married to her super awesome husband Donavan since 2001 and lives in Matthews, NC with their two ridiculously beautiful children.

Also by AnnaLisa Grant

Oxblood: A Victoria Asher Novel - 1

<u>The Lake Series</u>
The Lake
Troubled Waters
Safe Harbor
Anchored: A Lake Series Novella

FIVE

As I Am

99 Days

24298089R00138

Made in the USA
Columbia, SC
25 August 2018